FABULOUS BRIGHTON

AN ANTHOLOGY

FABULOUS BRIGHTON

Edited by

Elizabeth Counihan
Deirdre Counihan
Liz Williams

Shrew Press

Shrew Press
14 Queens Park Rise
Brighton
East Sussex
BN2 2ZF

First published by Shrew Press 2000

ISBN 0-9538481-0-8

Printed by KP Litho, 38 Gloucester Road, Brighton

FABULOUS BRIGHTON

ACKNOWLEDGEMENTS

The Editors would like to thank:

David Pringle for being our Consulting Editor. David is the Editor of Hugo Award winning Interzone, Britain's premier science fiction magazine.
David Kohn for his financial and marketing expertise.
Sally and Martin Hadwen for help with computer graphics.
The Montpelier Writers' Group for their enthusiastic support for the project
Stuart Grey (of Austin Grey Estate Agents) for sponsoring the project so generously.
Charles North for sponsoring the project and typesetting.
Peter Counihan for website design.
Nick Szczepanik for typesetting and design.
The staff of **Fullertons** for their help with photocopying.
Chris Atrell at KP Litho for invaluable technical assistance.

We would also like to thank **Deirdre Counihan** for the cover design.

Contents

Foreword

Simon Fanshawe

The planet 'what if...?' is a wonderful place to go. Sci-Fi, or Speculative Fiction as it's now called - New Labour, New Name presumably - is a dazzling feat of imagination. It is the literary form of possibility. It is essentially radical because it challenges us to embrace new worlds, how things might be, and to look beyond how things are. It is an affront to conservatism because it expands the ordinary into the extraordinary, old certainties into new potentials and turns convention on its head. SF is about nothing if not about change.

So the gathering of this group of local writers, some internationally known and some entirely new, is a perfect accompaniment to The Place To Be. The City Bid and the celebrations during the Year 2000 are, if you like, an exercise in speculation. It challenges the entire town to picture what we might be like in ten or fifteen years' time. What kind of place do we want to live in? What kind of town are we? What kind of city could we be? If we imagine we may achieve it.

The collection is also another example of the way that Brighton and Hove grips people creatively, how the town magically draws the imaginative to the coast and once they've revelled in the freedom to lie nude on the beach for a while, then shows them the word processor and tells them to get on with it. Our own 'slacker' economy is a hot bed of production. And so there appears to have grown a cluster of Speculative Fiction writers in town. They apparently meet. I assume it's in a bar that's like being on the set in Men In Black. A bar packed with beings with two heads, three shoulders, x-ray vision, alien make-up, scaly backs, wild colouring, staggering ability and intelligence and phenomenal powers. And no-one thinks odd of it. Pretty much like any bar in Brighton and Hove in other words. Of course there are these mad writers in town. There are few other places in Britain they wouldn't feel weird, because, let's face it, here an eye brow is more likely to be pierced than raised at the unusual.

With the writers Lynne Truss, Nick Szczepanik and Peter James leading the way, let's hope that in years to come Brighton and Hove sees the expansion of this coterie of fantasists whose everyday is the weird. Let's hope that this anthology builds on the success of the magazines Scheherazade and Interzone and makes Brighton and Hove in the future The Place To Be.....strange, The Place To Imagine......

The Green Man

Lynne Truss

In the haberdasher's on North Street, the miniature Mr Cope was considering emerald velvet and jade silk. Though he was obliged to stand on an upturned fish-crate to see properly over the counter, and the air in the shop was thick and hot (and a bit fishy, too) for such an indoor mission at midday in July, he seemed not to mind. He produced a monocle on an olive ribbon and peered at the fabrics more closely. There seemed to be just one concern preventing his final decision.

'Other colours?' he asked in a high, reedy voice, tapping the cloth with a fine long painted finger. 'Have you this stuff in other colours, Mr Moss?'

The shopkeeper exchanged glances with his brother, who was busily matching large buttons to chartreuse brocade. Was the question from the strangling dwarf some sort of trap? What large, goggly eyes he had! Rather like the Prince of Wales. The same long fingers, too. At Cope's imperious question, Moss frowned a request for guidance. His brother, quite as quick at facial semaphore, nodded smartly, his mouth drawn tight.

'Other colours, Mr Cope?' exclaimed Moss (who had once worked in the theatre). 'Why, heaven forfend! While other colours are of course pressed upon us by the vicissitudes of fashion, Mr Cope, my brother and I would be distraught beyond measure to allow anything to cross this counter that we could not in truth describe as verdant, viridescent, or just plain green.'

'Good.'

Mr Cope rubbed his chin and, turning, prepared to jump down from his rough platform. Then he stopped himself.

'So you would not,' he said, turning back to face the shopkeeper, 'For the sake of argument, and remembering that the town is a giddy seaside place full of people of uncertain taste whose reason is still easily unseated by thoughts of poor Nelson's untimely demise last autumn, entertain the notion of aquamarine?'

'Ah. Aquamarine?' Moss thought about it quickly. 'Alas not, Mr Cope. It went well in ninety-eight, of course. I cannot deny it. But for our present taste, it is too blue.'

'Too blue? Ha. Very well, very well.' Cope seemed satisfied, if oddly disappointed, too. 'Too blue!' He jumped down, and collected in the same motion the mint-green cocked hat he had placed upturned on the counter, with its mint-green gloves lightly folded on its rim. He had made his decision.

'I shall have a shirt of the jade, a suit of the emerald and a cloak of the chartreuse. I am content.'

Moss wrote down the order and smiled. He expected another question, and it was soon to come.

'We did not mention lime, Mr Moss.'

'Lime, Mr Cope?'

Moss, a tall man, was now obliged to look down on his customer, which was awkward. He fought the impulse to crouch.

'Suppose I wanted a suit of lime?' said Cope. 'For the Thursday ball? One might cut quite a dash in lime, don't you think?'

Moss bit his lip.

'Too yellow, Mr Cope. We would consider lime too yellow.'

'Well, well.' Cope produced a green handkerchief from his pocket and wiped his hands. It was a hot day. He looked tired. 'I shall recommend your excellent grasp of the spectrum to all the green men of my acquaintance, Mr Moss! What a splendid name you have, by the bye. I confess I am persuaded by such a name alone to give you all my business!'

Moss and his brother forced a polite laugh, wishing he would go. The Prince of Wales was expected shortly, and the shop was not large.

'I shall return for fittings on Tuesday. Good day.'

'Good day, sir.'

The little man left the shop and after the briefest hesitation outside (pulling his gloves on to his hands, despite the season), turned east downhill towards the Steyne. He limped slightly. Allowing an interval to pass, the Mosses stepped on to the street to watch him go. The two good haberdashers looked at each other and shuddered.

'He rubs the green stuff in a bit, doesn't he?' said the first.

'He certainly does,' said the second. 'What do you think of Bros Moss as a name, by the way?'

And so they thought no more about it. They knew they were in for a bonanza. It was July, the prince's birthday was a fortnight away, and Brighton trade thrived—then, as now—on the custom of loonies, no questions asked. Once the 'Green Man' was out of sight, the Mosses returned to their shop to pull the covers from their fashionable pinks, greys, blues, violets and mauves, and proceed with the rest of their day.

The Green Man had certainly not gone unnoticed in Brighton this summer of 1806, what with his notion of eating only green food (tricky during the meat course, but enormous fun in the avocado season) and restricting himself to green livery and wallpaper. In fact, future history books would record an extremely bad verse about this odd little figure, notable for the way in which a synonym for 'green' is not at any point attempted:

The Green Man

A spruce little man in a doublet of green
Perambulates daily the streets and the Stein.
Green striped his waistcoat, his small clothes are green,
And oft round his neck a green 'kerchief is seen.
Green watch string, green seals, and for certain I've heard,
(Tho' they're powdered) green whiskers and eke a green beard.
Green garters, green hose, and deny it who can,
The brains, too, are green of this little green man.

In some ways the timing of Cope's sojourn in Brighton was brilliant. With the Napoleonic Wars finally (apparently) at an end, England was a breezy, rattling, loose-limbed, bracing sort of place. Some rather good nature poetry was being written in Somerset and the north. There was lots of rich food. The architecture, furniture and ceramics were quite good. The novels of Jane Austen were just around the corner, leaf tea was sold at affordable prices, and the sea-dipping from bathing machines was absolutely great.

But there was a negative aspect to all this burgeoning of leisure activity and easy travel and ready self-expression, as Cope soon discovered. If you were a visitor from another planet who hoped to stand out in a crowd, setting yourself up as a little green man in Brighton in 1806 was hopeless. The harder you worked at cultivating a wild eccentricity and exhibiting your Martian credentials, the more you found yourself asked round for tea and buns. The more you screamed your foppish abhorrence of lime and aquamarine, the more you paradoxically revealed yourself to be a true Brightonian. When even the haberdashers humoured your monomania as a matter of routine courtesy, it was a sure sign that the novelty of your Martian beginnings was something that was never to be acknowledged.

'Dear all at station M12XZ,' wrote Cope in his first interplanetary letter home [his real name was not Cope, of course. It was Iggy to his friends, or M12XZ - nnnn in official documents]. 'Well, here I am! A little green man in a fashionable English seaside resort! Only a matter of time before the Brighton dwellers put two and two together. Unfortunately, these people are not quite finished with exploring their own planet yet, and are therefore disappointingly intrigued by the existence of little yellow men, little brown men, little red men and little—or rather, quite large, actually—black men. The idea of little green men hasn't yet occurred to them! However, when I tell them I have travelled 48 million miles to be here, I think they will fall back in amazement, don't you? After all, the Prince Regent has furnished his 'pavilion' in the style of China (and China is a mere few thousand miles away), and everyone makes a great fuss about that! Oh well. Give Tibby a stroke [Tibby's official name: M12XZ - ppprrr].'

Cope could be forgiven for expecting a bit of adulation on this visit. Previous Martians had had a fantastic reception on earth. Pyramids and earthworks had been erected to them all over the place. Although tourist Martians were strictly not permitted to ransack the planets they visited, back home on Mars, Cope's cousin Jed [or M12XZ - cdec] had a collection of smuggled Earth mementoes that Cope had for a long time envied and admired.

These ranged from the snapped-off arms of the Venus de Milo (interestingly complete with bucket) to the entire Colossus at Rhodes, minus feet.

'All these were given to me,' Jed often reminisced. 'Earth people are so innocent! So quick to revere the unusual! You will have a wonderful time among them, cousin! Go anywhere but Brighton, and I guarantee it!'

But Cope had somehow failed to absorb this last piece of advice, and was now playing the price for inattention. How could a true green Martian fail to make an impact anywhere on this planet known for its thirst for novelty? It didn't make sense. Yet it was true.

'There goes the little green man,' people on the Steyne might say, with a broad-minded distant smile. 'Oh but that spectral rigour riff he's into! Ugh, so boring! Have you been to hear the Savoyard musicians, by the way? I hear they're taking the place by storm!'

Cope tried a number of other attention-seeking ruses, but nothing worked. Talking to himself. Sitting in doorways on a blanket. Doing his hair in unusual ways. Affecting tassels. But weirder people turned up in Brighton every day, some of them with unusual breeds of dog, and Cope's greenness—however far he pushed it—simply could not compete. Finally, in desperation he jumped off the cliff outside his lodgings and got a report in the newspaper. But it was a cheap trick and he soon regretted it, especially as it resulted in a broken leg. True, he had made an impact at last, but unfortunately only on the shingle that broke his fall.

* * * * *

Having ordered his suit of clothes on that hot July day, the dejected Cope arrived limping at the Steyne unsure what to do next. He had run out of ideas. The Savoyards were playing. A long-haired aristocrat called Byron was parading a cross-dressing 'cousin' (it was a girl, dressed up). At the Pavilion, the Prince Regent was taking delivery of a new light fitting the size of Tunbridge Wells. It was no use competing with any of this. Cope sat down, got some grapes out of his pocket, and began to eat them dolefully, all the while weeping green tears.

'I have not come all this way to be ignored,' he declared aloud. 'No one would come all this way to be ignored.'

He followed his grapes with a leek, a few loose peas and an asparagus spear (all less than pleasant when raw), and then, after burping a deep green burp, dabbed his mouth with an eau-de-Nil napkin, still lost in self-pity. Which was when it happened. The Thing.

'Actually,' said a voice behind him. 'Although I hate to contradict you, cousin, I do come here to be ignored. In fact, we all do. Look at the stuff I get away with. It's fantastic.'

Cope looked up. It was the Prince Regent! Wearing the royal garter and powdered wig and everything! Cope was utterly confused. Had the Prince Regent just addressed him as 'cousin'? Or was this an hallucination caused by a long-anticipated chlorophyll overload?

'Didn't I advise you to go to Bognor, Iggy?' sighed the Regent. 'If you wanted celebrity for just being a Martian?'

Cope blinked a few times, swallowed, and tried to imagine what was going on. Just being a Martian? He felt weightless, as if back in space.

'Bognor?' he repeated, stupidly. 'Bognor isn't going yet, is it?'

'Bournemouth, then!' said the Regent. 'But I know I said Not Brighton!'

Cope's green lips quivered so much he couldn't say Bournemouth. He said 'Bor, bor, bor,' and then stopped. This was too weird, and quite frankly he wasn't yet certain the asparagus was blameless.

'Iggy, it's me!' snapped the Regent, impatiently. 'It's Jed! You mean you didn't guess?'

'I don't—' began Cope, and then stopped. He wanted to cry again, or at least to ask questions. But since whole sentences wouldn't come, he just tried out some promising beginnings. 'I—didn't,' he said, slowly. 'I—can't.' He paused. 'I'm—not.' And then he gave up. He fainted on the grass, which was both lucky and unlucky, since it suited his colour scheme exquisitely, but at the same time ensured nobody discovered him for hours.

* * * * *

The history books do not record what happened to Cope, but the truth is he remained in Brighton and suddenly—nobody quite knows why—started to make the best of its anonymity, instead of trying to impress people all the time. Possibly the place was full of other Martians, anyway—it would certainly explain a thing or two. So, whether the Prince Regent was indeed Jed in cunning disguise, or whether the momentous pep-talk was a mere biological by-product of an insufficiently masticated raw vegetable, the effect was the same. Cope's realisation that if he wanted to be starkly different from everybody else, Bournemouth or Bognor in a few years' time would fit the bill perfectly made all the blood (or possibly sap) in his little green body run cold.

He continued to wear green because it suited him. He shopped with the Mosses, and did not patronise the Whites or the Browns. Eccentricity for its own sake—that was the point of Brighton. Being a Martian and nobody minding. Coming 48 million miles and being ignored. You don't get that in Bognor. And whatever they tell you, you don't get that in bloody Bournemouth, either.

Sing a Song of Saxon

Nigel Brown

'You can't evict the Saxon Community. It's racial harassment!' Stan's words came out too soon, even before his visitor had fully stepped into his office. This was a bad beginning; his nerves had already let him down. The man looked startled at the outburst, but still reached across the councilman's office desk, hand outstretched over the flickering computer screen and the folded copy of Anglo-Saxon Chronicle.

'Councilman Stan?' he said, shaking Stan's hand vigorously, 'I'm Hugo Olsson.' He sat down opposite.

A Scandinavian name, Stan thought. A Viking name. 'My full title is Ealdorman Aethelstan,' he replied. 'I'm the leader of the Saxon Community in Brighton.'

'Ah... Aethelstan. May I call you Stan? After all, this is the twenty-first century. We shouldn't stand too much on formalities.' Without waiting for a reply, Olsson continued. 'And let's not use the word *racial* at this point, shall we? I'd prefer to think of your claims in terms of descent from particular... ancestors.' He smiled with satisfaction, revealing large tombstone teeth. Stan noticed his long, pallid face had a youthful boyish look spoiled by pockmarked skin. A pockmarked Viking, he thought. The old enemy.

'The landlord, Anderson Development Corporation, has engaged me to act on their behalf,' Olsson said.

'You're a lawyer?' Stan interrupted, nervously. He could feel sweat breaking out underneath his headband. He shifted uncomfortably in his pinstriped suit. He hated wearing it, but it was necessary to look as respectable as possible.

'I'm an historian,' Olsson said. 'My interest is in post-Roman, pre-Norman British history. I'm based at York University, but I've been asked to come to Brighton and sort this little problem out.'

'This 'little problem' is my community's existence,' Stan replied coldly.

'Ah yes!' Olsson said. 'Please, forgive me. I mean no offence. I take that on board. I'm merely here to establish some facts.'

'Go on,' said Stan. He thought he could see where this was leading to. The Saxons of Brighton had been down this route before.

'Your claim on the North Laines area is based on your... ethnic identity, I'd suppose we'd call it. The landlords have some doubts as to that; I'm here to support their conviction that the so-called Saxon community in Brighton has no racial basis, and therefore no claim.'

'We've been here since our forefathers, led by Aelle, landed on the Sussex coast in 497,' Stan growled. 'The Saxons are lost in history... everywhere but in Brighton. Brighton was founded by the Saxon Brithelm. The original name for it was 'Brithelmston'. 'Tun' is a homestead. This is still our home. Our tenant rights derive from the 'Brithelm Statute' made when Brithelm himself found...personal favour with the local bishop.'

Olsson raised his eyebrows. 'Personal, eh?' he remarked. 'Some things in Brighton never change. You mean he was -'

Stan felt his cheeks growing hot. 'The facts are in the City Museum. I'll direct you there on your way out.'

'I hear what you say, Councillor,' Olsson said. He smiled. 'A cultural continuation is not the same as an ethnic group, however. The Law makes a distinction on this; just because you call yourself Saxons doesn't make you Saxons. I can sing a Saxon song. I'm no Saxon.' His teeth gleamed with his grin. 'Let me illustrate this point.'

Olsson stood up, and strode to the large bay window which looked down onto the City Square. Stan joined him. Stan's office was two flights up in the civic building. From this height, they could see across the square, down Market Street to the entrances of the labyrinthine Lanes. The streets were full of pedestrians; office workers, tourists, and a small group gathered in one corner of the square, busking with lutes.

'Look,' Olsson said. He pointed down at the buskers. Stan could identify them by their beige woven tunics and cloaks. The men wore beards like he did, as a mark of his identity, but they lacked the headbands of his folk. 'Are those your people?'

Two women and a child joined the buskers.

'Penny for the poor!' the child called out to a group of Japanese tourists. His shrill voice could be heard echoing around the square. 'Starvin' we are!'

'No,' Stan told Olsson. 'Those country tramps aren't any relation to my community. They're wood colliers, charcoal burners, who reckon the pickings are good in Brighton. They've been coming in to the city these last few weeks, claiming Saxon kinship.' It angered him to see the filthy group bringing the name of his noble people into disrepute. After Olsson, they were the next problem on his agenda.

'I agree,' said Olsson. 'They've made a camp outside the city, but I'm not going to bother with it. I'm more concerned with your Saxon claims, not theirs.' His gaze fell on Stan's desk. 'Isn't that a copy of your community newspaper?'

Olsson picked it up. It was open on the Riddle page. He read out the one which had been ringed in red ink:

'Living, yet unborn,
Holding memories, yet no mind,
Indestructible, yet so soft,
Married to it, yet no church bind,
What has the Aetheling left behind?'

Olsson looked unimpressed. 'I know that riddles figured strongly in old Saxon culture. They sound trite to the modern ear.'

Stan took the paper from him. 'We value them,' he said stiffly. 'They can hold truths that the ignorant miss completely!'

Olsson shrugged, then settled back into his chair.

'Our Saxon identity hasn't been questioned before,' Stan continued. 'The City of Brighton accepts it.' He waved his arm around the office. 'I'm here as a representative of my people, here, in the City Hall. I am empowered by ancient right to adjudicate amongst the Saxons, covering everything from property rights to marriages, even for property rights granted by marriages!'

'I would never dispute that with you, but that's not the issue here,'

Olsson replied. 'Am I not correct in understanding that your position at the City Hall, as councilman, is due to an election in the North Laines electoral ward? Where your supporters have a majority?' He chuckled. 'It doesn't prove anything, really.'

Stan glared at him. 'You can't evict us.'

'The landlords own the freehold of the North Laines. You know the Council sold it off last year to raise funds for the city. As landlords, they have the right to pull down... slums.' Before Stan could react to that, Ollson leaned forward and lowered his voice. 'It's very exciting. You know some archaeological digging was undertaken at the bottom of Trafalgar Street, before the new car park was laid out?'

Stan had been aware of it. He grunted, non-committedly.

'Evidence of a Viking shipyard was found. In Southern England! The landlords want to create this, for the City of Brighton.' He threw a detailed plan across Stan's desk with a flourish.

Stan stared at it in horror. Ollson's voice confirmed the unbelievable scenario before him. 'The developers plan to dig out an old creek of the river, there.' He stabbed a finger down on the plan, at Trafalgar Street. 'Call it the Trafalgar Basin. We demolish along here...' his finger pushed along Cydney Street and beyond, knocking down all the buildings, the shops and homes of the Saxon Community, '... and replace this area with bakeries, antique and craft shops, all on a new theme. A Viking theme.' He grinned ferociously. 'My home town York's Viking Centre has proved a great success. This will be a larger development, nearer to London, Europe...

'But…' Stan struggled for words. 'We have craft shops there already, and bakeries!'

Ollson shook his head sorrowfully. 'I'm an historian, Councillor, but although my eyes are often focused on the Past, that's taught me that nothing stands still. Things... people... move on. The landlords feel that the present North Laines area needs renovation, and the City agrees with them. This will be an attractive addition to Brighton. London's St.Catherine's Dock near Tower Bridge, the Albert Dock in Liverpool... the people of Brighton deserve the same thing. This is their opportunity to have it. The landlords are being reasonable, despite your attitude. Your associates can rent shop units in the new development.' He sat back, relaxed, and peered at Stan through arched, slim fingers.

'You know we'll never be able to afford new rents in a place like that!' Stan said. He had no doubt that the landlords would offer lower rents to shops selling Viking trinkets. His mouth was dry, but he managed to croak out the threat that his father had used so successfully before, in previous disputes. 'You can't evict the Saxon Community,' he repeated. 'I still call it racial harassment.' He sat back, having played his trump card once more.

Olsson seemed to expect it. 'Of course. I'm in tune with you, there. It is *racial* descent, you claim? Most probably from the Saxon folk found buried in the graveyard excavated last year?'

Stan nodded. He could sense a trap, but he could not deny this foundation-stone of the community's belief. Olsson reached into his briefcase, and produced a small, shiny spatula.

'I've organised DNA testing of those old Saxon bones, and the laboratory -quite independent! - has managed to isolate enough genetic markers to identify any modern day descendents of those buried Saxons.' He waved the spatula before Stan's hypnotised eyes. 'I just need a skin scraping from your inner cheek. It's quite harmless. Anthropologists are doing this all the time, now. This will settle the matter.'

The trap was sprung. Stan knew he could not refuse. A Court Order would surely follow if he did. Yet he felt reluctant to scientifically test his people's origins. There was a nugget of doubt in the back of his mind, based mainly on stories of intermarriage in the plague years when the Saxon community had been devastated like so many others. Added to that, the influx of visitors to Brighton in the Regency Years had taken their toll. He knew there were even conversions to Saxon kinship in his own family, way back. He hesitated.

'Just one sample from me won't constitute proof,' he objected.

'It's a start. If you cannot even begin to provide the evidence, I can assume you are not racial descendents of the original Saxons,' Olsson said, an he moved to put the spatula away.

'No!' Stan exclaimed, red-faced. 'We are! Do this test, if it will satisfy you.' He felt the urge to show this smug outsider the reality of Saxon life in Brighton. 'We're Saxons. Come here, to City Hall tomorrow night. It's our annual Salvation Feast. We traditionally perform riddles, after the meal. Maybe you'll learn something there!' The moment he said the words, he regretted it.

'Thank you,' Olsson said, looking pleased, even impressed. 'An opportunity to meet the North Laines Saxon Trading Community will be useful, before it's disbanded.' He smiled, and Stan noticed Olsson's teeth were cracked at the bottom, and flecked with slime. 'My *cultural* historical research will benefit, I'm sure. Besides, we'll have the results of the genetic test by then. You can make the appropriate announcement before your...associates.'

Stan sat quiet for a long time, after Olsson had departed. He recalled the words of Beortric, his late father's oldest friend.

'I'm sure you'll do as well as your father Ceolmund would have.'

The memory haunted him now, as did the grim, worn expressions on the other traders' faces. Like them, he wished his father still led the community in this time of crisis. But it was up to him, now. He had to stop the evictions. He knew the Saxons would never survive dispersal amongst the cosmopolitan sprawl of Brighton. They would lose their distinct identity; disappear into the population as had happened over the rest of modern

Britain. Stan was happy to live in a multi-cultural society, but he believed that it meant his traditional Saxon way of life had a place in it as well.

He felt a traitor to his kin for giving the mouth sample to be tested. A wretched fool. He knew he had let his pride trip him up, and he hated himself for it. His father would have stalled for time; refused to do the test. It was too late now. The telephone rang. It was Judith, his wife.

'Do you know where Hilde is?' she asked. 'She was supposed to help me at home this afternoon.' Stan found himself reassuring her, although he felt despair. He guessed where their daughter had disappeared to. This was all he needed.

He plucked the Anglo-Saxon Chronicle off his desk, and scrutinised the riddle Olsson had read out. Hilde had sent him the paper, it was she who wanted him to see the riddle. Her boy-friend Leo had written it.

The morning had begun badly for Stan at home, even before the eviction notice had arrived. Hilde had announced that Leo wished to read his riddle out at the Salvation Feast that night. As Ealdorman, it was Stan who had the last word on the performances. But Leo was one of the wood colliers. A country tramp. Hilde had scoffed at Stan's pleas for Saxon solidarity, his appeals for her to remember her heritage, her position as the daughter of the Saxon Ealdorman. His car was up at the North Laines. He left his office and hurried down to the Steine river. Not the shortest route home, but the best way to avoid other Saxons, that morning. He had to think this through, before any explanations were due.

The riverwalk, with its pink and white cherry blossom trees, was beautiful in April, but he could not enjoy the sight of their petals fluttering onto the streaming water, or stop to contemplate them as they swirled down towards the Steine Bridge and the sea. He followed a yellow blaze of rippling daffodils, along the bankside, until he reached Trafalgar Street; the northern boundary of the Saxon enclave. Leaving the riverside, the route soon took him into the heart of the North Laines.

Once in Cydney Street, between the rows of terraced houses, his nostrils filled with the smell of bacon sizzling in pans at a take-away stall. The turmoil in his mind became stilled by the familiar cries of the market traders the shuffling through the crowds, the buzz and hum of Saxon life: the kinship of his tribe. The screech of a seagull caught his attention. He spotted it, perched high up on the straw thatched roof. The Saxons lived on the first floors, behind walls made of split tree trunks. Below were the shops, fronted by stalls - the livelihoods he had now helped Olsson to destroy.

Pushing between two of the stalls, he skirted by a group of tourists and locals. They were gathered around a corn-grinding demonstration run by his cousin Edith. She glanced up at him; an unspoken query in her worried eyes. He averted his gaze, his cheeks burning with embarrassment.

A group of American tourists were posing outside his shop, *Saxon Centuries*, by the life-size statue of Brithelm which stood in the centre of the street. Arm raised, sword pointing to the sky, Brithelm's other hand clasping his horn; the sight had always been an inspiration to Stan. Days of glory and conquest, he thought wistfully.

'I know where Hilde is,' he told Judith when he entered the shop. 'I won't be long.'

'How did the meeting go?' she called out, but he was already through the shop, out in the yard and starting up his car. He drove his Peugeot 205 up the London road, towards the outskirts of Brighton. The road followed alongside the river for a mile, before the Steine disappeared upstream into a tunnel which delved deep into the chalk uplands behind Brighton.

Stan dreaded what he would find at Leo's home. The local paper had published a few reports, but they had been mostly about the problem the council had of finding a permanent location for the camp, not about the camp's conditions. When he turned off the road, near the little Henge past Patcham, he was shocked at the sight. There were no caravans, beaten-up trucks and cars, as he had expected. A number of wooden huts covered the field, with men, women and children going about their business between them. He stopped his field gate, and got out.

Stan still wore his pin-striped suit. He thought of rolling up his trouser legs, to avoid the mud, but decided that would look even worse. Gingerly, he opened the gate and picked his way between piles of heaps of rotting vegetation towards the huts. A hubbub reached his ears; the bleating of goats, the cluck of chickens, the chatter of men as they carried bundles of twigs over to a charcoal pit at the centre of the camp. Stan found himself entranced by the sight of the nimble finger movements of a woman working a loom. He had a similar machine in his shop, but it had fallen into disrepair. Judith preferred to buy their clothes from BHS.

'It's cool, isn't it Dad?'

Hilde. She stood outside the nearest hut, holding hands with Leo. Now that Stan was closer, he could see that the hut wall was made of the familiar split tree trunks, and the roof was an untidy thatch of straw. It was larger than at first sight, as it had been built over a pit in the ground.

'What are you doing here?' he asked, although he knew the answer.

'We want to be together,' Hilde said. She looked up at Leo, and Stan recognised her expression: the same one his wife gave him in their tender moments. He realised that he would be losing two arguments today.

'But what is this?' Stan pointed at the huts, the mud. 'What is here that the North Laines can't offer you?'

'This is the Green way of life, Dad,' Hilde replied. 'Back to nature... away from the pollution of the city.' She looked at his sorrowful expression, and her face softened. 'I'm not going anywhere else. The people here have stopped travelling. They say they've come home.'

'It's true, Ealdorman,' Leo said. 'I'll not be taking her away from her folk.'

Stan looked at the young man with new respect. He seemed to read a father's deepest anxieties.

'I want you at the Salvation Feast tomorrow,' Stan said. 'It's important.'

She nodded. 'If Leo can come. Did you read the riddle?' She grinned. 'Did you guess the answer?' He considered her request. The scandal of the Ealdorman's daughter would keep many a gossip going, but he knew he had no real choice.

'Both come,' he said. 'It's gone beyond riddles, anyway.'

On the way back to the car, mulling over how he would explain this to Judith, he was surprised to find a four-legged animal cross his path, snuffling. It was a small pig.

The pig came back to his mind as he sat the next night at the High Table, facing a roasted half-carcass of pork. His people considered them lucky. His traditional Saxon helmet even had a little metal model of one on top, but he knew its value as a lucky charm had deserted him. The Salvation Feast was usually the highlight of the Saxon calendar. This year, the subdued community sat at three long tables, filling the magnificent Brighton City Hall with a murmur of conversation in the flickering yellow candlelight.

Stan surveyed his community with a miserable eye. They did not deserve their troubles, they did not deserve a fool like him as their leader. Beortric the cloth-weaver, sitting with his family, caught his eye raised a glass of mead. Stan looked down at the table, and poked at his and cabbage disheartedly.

'Cheer up, Ealdorman,' said Judith. She gazed at him with worried eyes, leaned forward and carved a piece of succulent pork for his plate. 'Hilde said she'd come.'

Stan smiled weakly at her, but he had lost what little appetite he had. He spotted Hugo Olsson entering the hall, at the back. Their Viking enemy strolled up the aisle, towards the dais.

'Is that him?' asked Judith.

Stan nodded. His throat was dry.

'I don't know how he had the cheek to accept your invitation to the Feast,' she sniffed.

Stan knew this was a rebuke for inviting the man in the first place, but he was glad he had done so. It proved that the Saxon people were generous to their enemies, they could stand and look them in the eye.

Olsson reached the dais, ignoring the curious looks from the diners. He stepped up onto the platform, and strode past the other Thanes seated at the top table.

'Councillor,' Olsson said. 'Thank you for inviting me here.' He looked at Judith, who stared coldly at him. 'You must be Mrs... er. Good evening.' She gave a slight nod.

'I'll not be here long,' he said, looking from his vantage point down the Hall. The whole community was present, all dressed in traditional Saxon dress - tunics, trousers, leather cross-garters, jewellery. Some of the men even wore small helmets; had round wooden shields and spears beside them.

'Interesting,' Olsson said. 'I see your shields have the old Saxons' central raised bosses, to deflect swords and axes. It'll take more than them to fend off eviction notices!'

'We call it the Salvation Feast because we thank the Lord for our presence in this land, still a distinct people after all these years,' said Stan.

'Ah,' Olsson replied. 'That reminds me...' He reached into an inner pocket, and drew out a piece of paper. 'Look at this.'

Stan read the letter, then closed his eyes to block out the damning words.

'The test confirms a lack of genetic markers, Councillor. You may be cultural Saxons, but you're not a racial group.'

Judith frowned. 'What does he mean, Stan?'

'I'm sorry, Judith,' he whispered, opening his eyes and staring down the hall, into nothingness. All was lost. As leader of this community it had been his lot to ease its destruction. He wondered if the City Council could house them all together - perhaps to start again - but he knew that was impossible. A thousand and a half years of tradition had come to an end.

'Here's Hilde!' his wife exclaimed. 'With Leo.' She glanced at him, to gauge his reaction, but it did not seem to matter anymore to him. The other Saxons could think what they wanted of Hilde's betrothal to a charcoal burner; they would all soon be tramps.

He felt a tap on his shoulder. 'Listen, Stan,' Olsson whispered in his 'I can offer you a shop unit in the new development... let's call it rent for your co-operation.'

Puzzled, Stan turned and stared at the man. Olsson grinned back, his yellow teeth glowing in the candlelight. Stan searched his face for a but he could see no reason for the Viking's sudden change of heart.

'Will you do it?' Olsson asked. 'I need to settle this today. I don't want trouble.'

Hilde came to the dais, but Leo hung back.

Then something unexpected happened: Stan noticed Leo nod at Olsson, as if they had previously met. Stan looked sharply at Olsson, but his expression gave nothing away. Thinking hard, Stan realised where Olsson would know Leo from. Why had Olsson bothered to follow it up, when he said he wouldn't? The thought struck a hollow chord inside him - reminded him of the devastating confirmation that he was no longer of pure Saxon blood. Suspecting it and knowing it were two different things. Suspicions could be suppressed, made to seem unimportant speculation. Facts could not be so easily ignored, especially if Olsson would not let him forget it. Yet this made Olsson's offer all the more mysterious.

'Why me?' he whispered. 'If I'm not a true Saxon anymore?'

'These people here will listen to you,' Olsson replied. 'If you explain the situation, they'll leave the North Laines quietly. You, yourself, can continue your life in this area,' Olsson said. 'Maybe establish a better one. At least they'll still be a cultural Saxon presence in Brighton.'

Stan felt his stomach churn. The Viking was right. Olsson's offer could

be the only chance for Saxon life to continue in the City of Brighton. He could remain here, together with his family. He looked at his wife, then his daughter, then at Leo.

Leo. He knew what he must do. Unsteadily, he got to his feet. The hall grew quiet, and expectant faces turned to him.

'Leo,' he called. 'Come up here.'

The young man was startled, but he stepped forwards, and climbed up onto the stage.

'I stand here before you as Ealdorman,' Stan began. As he continued, his voice grew stronger, gained in conviction. 'For those of us here who may not know,' he glanced at Olsson, who looked confused, 'the word can mean 'Judge' as well as 'Leader'. As such, by our Saxon Law...' he reached out and took Leo's hand, together with Hilde's, and held them up together, 'at this Folk Moot of our people, I marry these two before the Lord, and our people.'

Gasps and cries, yet most of the Saxons, he was pleased to see, were smiling benevolently. Hilde's face was burning red. A few people began to clap. Old Beortric the cloth-weaver raised another cup of mead to him, and winked. 'To Ceolmund's boy!' he cried. The words recalled memories for Stan: years of standing proud next to his father at earlier Salvation Feasts, toasting prosperity. Good, happy times. He saw now that the community was on the brink of destruction, but also that its plight gave them a tremendous advantage, one which he was determined to take -they now had nothing to lose. If he was wrong in his intuition, he knew in his heart that even his father would have been proud of the courage he was about to display.

'I haven't finished yet!' Stan called out. 'As a wedding present, I give Leo a share in my tenancy... and in my property rights in the North Laines!'

The audience was in an uproar. Leo and Hilde stood before them, stunned by his words. He sat down with a thump, exhausted.

'Do you know what you've done?' Judith hissed in his ear. He drained his cup of mead, then thumped the table with it until there was silence. Once more, he struggled to his feet.

'Saxon tradition demands riddles after a feast.' Stan turned to Leo. 'Before that, you have a tale, Leo. It's time for us all to hear it.' His glance at Olsson's grim expression told him this gamble would pay off.

Leo looked out over the crowd. 'My name is Leo,' he began. 'Short for Leofwine. My people are Brithelm's Saxons too, but we left the Brighton area in 1066 when William of Normandy began to ransack the land. We made a life for ourselves in the deep fastness of the Weald Forests, and as time went by the plague, then the French raids along the coast gave us no reason to return.

'This last year we've returned to the coast, to claim our rightful lands. We've kept quiet up until now, as we hoped we could return and join back with our kinfolk here without bringing too much attention to ourselves. We've survived for so long as a separate people by doing that. I see now that the time has come to 'come out of the forest', as my people say.'

'Ridiculous!' It was Olsson. 'That will never stand up in English Law!'

Stan turned to him. 'Maybe not,' he said, 'But I'm willing to bet that your precious genetic marker test will prove Leofwine's story. *His* people have remained isolated in the Weald. I believe...' he gulped, 'they're more Saxon than the rest of us.' Several of the men cried out in angry protest, but he held up his hand until they were quiet.

'That's the point,' Stan continued. 'Brighton has had a long tradition of harbouring immigrants and dissenters. The Celts welcomed the Romans. The Romans welcomed us. I'm sure the Council will welcome these people here.' He fixed Olsson with his pale, blue eyes. 'If the landlords protest at this, I'm sure we can find lawyers who would be prepared to take our case to the European Court of Human Rights. That will take time - years. And time is money.

'I'm sorry, Olsson,' Stan continued, 'but you gave yourself away. I realised it when I noticed that you'd met Leofwine before. You must have visited the camp, heard their story, and believed it. That's why you made me that offer when you saw Leofwine here. You thought I knew the story too, and that I believed it. You thought you could pay me off. You were too clever, but you didn't know about Leofwine and Hilde.' Olsson scowled.

'I told you that a riddle can hold a truth inside it, Olsson,' Stan said. 'Can you recite it, Leo?'

Leo stood on the dais, and turned to address the expectant faces. He recited:

Nigel Brown

'Living, yet unborn,
Holding memories, yet no mind,
Indestructible, yet so soft,
Married to it, yet no church bind,
What has the Aetheling left behind?'

'I saw the solution to your riddle, Leo,' Stan said. 'It's the land, isn't it? This land you left behind. That's the answer to both of our problems.'

Turning to Olsson, he continued: 'I propose an old solution to this new situation. A line is to be drawn here, in Brighton. You keep your Viking centre in York; your plans for anywhere else as well. Let that be under the Danelaw. Here, in Brighton, we'll remain Saxon - as we always have.'

The Viking drew a breath; jeers began to fill the room. Stan nodded in the direction of the door. Olsson strode out, his head aloof, his face pinched in disdain. Brithelm's Saxons of Brighton began to cheer their leader.

Doctor Theo's Excellent Tonic

Paul Laville

1.

'We're here, boy!' announced square-jawed Captain Bain.

Harish Patel was confused. They'd only been sailing for ten turbulent minutes out of Brighton. Here? Where?

'You said you wanted to find your fiancee,'said the Captain.

Harish nodded.

'Well this came from here,' said Bain, picking up a small, salt-encrusted green bottle, shaped like an inverted T, from an old, wooden locker nailed into the cabin floor. The wrap-around label had worn away and the bottle's square neck had been smashed off. Harish had found it like that in Rebecca's room at the University residence.

Captain Bain lobbed it at Harish, who just about caught it.

'Show me that note again,' he asked.

Harish gave him the note he had found inside the bottle. The Captain unfurled it and read out loud what it said.

'Artefact from grid four: 150m. November 29th 2000. Some kind of Well under the sea. People? Got to get closer to this Doctor Theo if he exists??? Put on the charm with Bain, see if he'll take me. Hah! Splendid girl! She didn't meet me, though I waited...'

Rebecca was studying Marine Biology and had presumably picked the bottle up from one of her journeys down to the seabed. But what else had she found down there, and did it have anything to do with her disappearance? This is what Harish had to find out. Rebecca had been gone for over three weeks and people were very worried.

The Captain said

'If she's mixed up with Doctor Theo she'll be here somewhere.'

'Doctor who?'

'Theo. A powerful man. That's a bottle of his renowned Excellent Tonic, which allegedly cures all ills, heals all wounds, refreshes the parts other mixers can't quite reach *etcetera etcetera*. He owns a spa - huge old building over in Queen's Park. You should start there. If your girlfriend was looking for Doctor Theo, that's where she'll have gone.'

Harish frowned.

'Queen's Park? So ... we're still in Brighton then?'

'Ah, but it's not the same Brighton. We've sailed sideways, lad. Poltice!' he yelled, opening the flimsy wooden door and shouting down into the snow. 'Poltice!'

A stooped, wrinkled man wearing a gauze coat and a stormhat, took form through the blizzard and entered the cabin like a ghost.

'Yes, Captain sir?' the apparition coughed.

'See the boy ashore.'

'Aye, Sir,' answered Poltice.

Harish thanked the Captain and followed Poltice outside.

2.

Poltice lowered a boarding ramp across to the quayside.

'One thing, young feller,' he said to Harish. 'We sail home on the time tide, so make sure you're back here before seven thirty tonight, understand? Not a minute later, else we'll sail without ye.'

Harish nodded: *Whatever*, then turned and walked carefully across the ramp, buttoning his duffel coat up to his chin.

The quayside was slippy with ice, and he kept his eyes on his feet all the way along it until he found the steps zig-zagging down to the promenade. Once on solid ground he looked up.

'Oh my God,' he whispered.

It was Brighton, and it was different.

At ground level cars, taxis, buses (and trams of the strangest designs Harish had ever seen) chased each other across the wide road. Stained black with filth and grime every vehicle spouted clouds of exhaust into the chilly air as though waging war on the falling snow. The statues and gargoyles crowning the baroque hotels rising high into the air, were thick with it.

Giant billboards loomed wherever he looked, a lot of them advertising 'Doctor Theo's Excellent Tonic', where a distinguished-looking gentleman with a curling moustache and patent leather hair held out a bottle of 'Excellent Tonic' to small boys and women. The theme was even carried over into the gaudy Christmas decorations lining the Promenade.

So this really is a parallel Brighton, Harish said to himself, feeling a long way from his home in south London, a long way from his Uncle's supermarket where, until yesterday, he worked.

Something boomed in the sky. Looking upwards he gasped in awe as a leviathan of the heavens emerged through the clouds: a monstrous, bloated bullet moving slowly, high above the town and out towards the sea. Attached to its underbelly was a long, brass-coloured gondola, from which people behind large windows waved at the ground. It was a great airship driven by four giant screw-type propellers which made the whole town reverberate with a bone-crunching thud-thud-thud-thud.

As the airship steered away Harish made a move for the Palace Pier, which he could see glittering in the near distance. It was a good landmark from which to begin his search. He hurried on.

A crossing on the kerb was indicated by a towering roadside lamppost surmounted by a large red globe. There was another opposite, and he stood with a gathering crowd of pedestrians waiting, he hoped, for it to change colour. The red globes turned green and the traffic stopped, just as a nearby clock chimed twelve.

Harish darted into the road, however, there was a scream, the pedestrians parted and he was suddenly exposed.

'Stop that man!' someone shouted.

A man with wild grey hair and rolling white eyes, ran straight at Harish. His face was covered in shiny silver scales, and he roared like a madman.

'Bloody hell!' cried Harish.

A thin man appearing from nowhere lifted a gold-coloured blunderbuss to his bottle-top spectacles, squinted along a sight, and fired.

People screamed and ducked.

The madman rammed his bulk into Harish's left shoulder and knocked him into the kerb. Looking up from the roadside, teeth clenched as a horrendous pain exploded from his shoulder, Harish saw that the thin man was joined by another man, shorter, fatter, with bushy black whiskers spraying out from under his top hat and his chubby cheeks.

The two men caught the madman and wrestled him to the ground.

'You're going to kill them!' screamed the madman.

'Hold him, Mr Stanley!' hissed the thin man to his fat companion.

'I've got him, Mr Shottick!'

Mr Stanley grabbed the madman's legs but still he struggled.

'Come on, Baxter,' growled Mr Shottick. 'Don't cause a scene.'

Losing his trilby in the struggle, Mr Shottick gagged Baxter with a grey cloth, produced a pair of iron manacles from inside his cape, and fastened them to the big man's wrists. Harish watched in horror.

Now Mr Shottick stared at Harish, noticing him for the first time. He looked as though he might say something, when a box-like black cab pulled up on the roadside belching noxious green fumes from its vertical twin exhaust pipes. The double doors on the cab flapped open and Harish shivered.

'Get him inside, Mr Stanley,' shouted Mr Shottick, turning his attention away from Harish. The two men bundled Baxter into the dark interior of the cab, from within which Harish thought he could see someone else, sitting quietly in green-hued shadow. Baxter screamed under his gag and kicked out, fighting the pull of the interior. But the cab seemed to suck the man inside. There was a truncated scream. Harish's ears popped, and suddenly it was quiet. When he peered inside the cab he could see nothing of Baxter.

Mr Shottick picked his trilby off the pavement and dusted it down, staring straight at Harish.

'Young man,' he said in a strangely formal Hindustani dialect Harish could not place. 'How did you get here?'

Harish backed away slowly, holding his shoulder. Mr Stanley, in English, snapped,

'Who is your master?'

Harish blinked.

'My master?'

A voice, deep, menacing, issued from the black/green darkness of the cab.

'What is it?'

'An escapee,' said Mr Stanley. 'His master will be discovered and fined. As for the boy...'

Impulsively Harish turned and ran.

'After him!'

Harish bolted across the road, dodging the swerving cars and trams which hooted and honked after him, and stumbled into a side street, throwing gawpers out of his way.

'Come back!' one of his pursuers shouted, sounding just like his uncle when Harish had stormed out of the shop yesterday evening, determined never to return.

Just keep on going, he told himself now as then. Keep on going and don't look back. All he had was Rebecca, and he wasn't going to let either his uncle or these people stop him from finding her.

So he ran, as fast as he could, turning into one alley, then into another, sprinting across a main road and heading left up a winding, cobbled street.

He emerged onto a wide, busy highway. There was a scream of car horns. He was running across a snow-frosted boulevard, a magnificent avenue of splendour and pomp glittering with Christmas lights. But, rearing hundreds of feet into the snowfall, dehumanising everything below them, were a series of black, stone arches, along which he could hear trains rumbling like thunder. The Festive Spirit didn't seem to extend into those dreadful shadows. He stopped on a traffic island and gasped for breath. Grand Parade, he thought to himself, or at least, this Brighton's equivalent.

There was no sign of Mr Stanley or Mr Shottick through the crowds, so he crossed the road, hugging his throbbing shoulder, and hid in a shop doorway. Someone nearby was roasting chestnuts, he could smell them. He had forgotten how hungry he was. But he had to keep his mind focused on Rebecca. He had to find her. She was his life, his soul. He could not live without her. It was just like the old stories. If he was Vishnu then she was Sri Lakshmi, sitting on a water-borne lotus flower which he had to swim upriver to reach. And like the old stories he had to overcome the obstacles thrown in his path. If he wanted her, then he had to fight for her, put his life in danger, perhaps even sacrifice himself for her.

But I'll do it, he told himself. *If she's here I'll find her.*

However, he wasn't too familiar with the real Brighton, let alone this one. He would have to ask someone if they knew where Queens Park was.

'We've lost him!' shouted Mr Shottick.

Mr Stanley came up behind him, mopping his face with a handkerchief.

'At least we got Baxter,' he panted. 'If he had gone into the sea village and warned them what the Doctor had planned...'

'My dear fellow,' interrupted Mr Shottick testily, 'the sea people can do nothing. When the Doctor introduces the new distillation of Tonic into the Well they will all die.'

'Then why go to all this trouble to recover him?'

Mr Shottick smiled. 'The Doctor wishes to punish him for destroying the barrels we loaded this morning.'

'We'll be loading again, I presume,' muttered Mr Stanley.

'I believe so,' answered Mr Shottick, scanning Grand Parade. 'But the distillation is now stored in one of the underground fuel tanks. Number three I believe.'

The box-like black cab pulled up alongside them and the doors opened.

'Doctor Theo,' said Mr Shottick humbly bowing to the dark interior. 'I am afraid the boy has eluded us.'

'Never mind the boy. Get in. You too, Stanley.'

The two men entered the cab, and the doors closed. Belching fumes, the cab joined the flow of traffic, and vanished .

3.

Harish wandered glumly through the streets of Brighton, hopelessly lost. When he asked people where Queens Park was they all seemed to tell him clear instructions, but over the past few hours he had found himself passing through a steamy Chinese quarter packed with restaurants and laundry-houses, had walked through several markets and had stumbled time and again upon the Promenade, meaning he was back where he had started. Nor could he buy food because his money was no good.

And all the time the minutes, the hours were ticking away.

In his mind's eye Harish could see his uncle and his father shaking their heads in shame. Such a useless stupid boy, they said. He had thrown away his career at University, and he was useless even in the shop. He couldn't stack shelves without dropping something, or push a trolley without tripping. He'd get lost in the stockroom and how old was he? 20?

Tut tut tut.

At least Rebecca believed in him. But where was she?

Rebecca Cloud looked up from her chains at the blonde, buxom Mary Jane who dripped water from her bathing suit onto Rebecca's faded denim jeans.

'Why do you give Mr Shottick such a hard time?' Mary Jane asked. 'You're spoiling it for everybody.'

The other girls splashed about in the pools, their laughter echoing around the high-vaulted chamber decorated with organic Art Nouveau motifs.

'Don't you see what he's doing to us? Rebecca answered. Look at you. You swim in that tonic stuff and you're changing, developing - what are they? Gills? And the scales on your hands, webbed feet…'

'It's the waters that are *stopping* the change,' Mary Jane said quietly, 'slowing it down at least.'

'That's a lie.'

Mary Jane hunkered down. 'Mr Shottick told us the Doctor has found a dilution that will change us back to normal.'

'That's an even bigger lie!'

'You'll see. He's taking us there tonight.' She smiled. 'Jhavesh said he'll be there.'

'Your boyfriend? That idiot servant?'

'At least he's here for me,' snapped Mary Jane.

Mr Shottick entered through an oval-shaped doorway, accompanied by a number of Indian servants bearing fine clothes. Mary Jane's boyfriend, Jhavesh, was one of them. They smiled at each other lovingly.

'Get dressed,' ordered Mr Shottick as the girls climbed out of the pool. He walked across to Rebecca, looked down at her. 'Have you reconsidered your decision not to bathe?'

'What are you going to do, Shottick? Throw me in?'

The thin man smiled.

'Unless you bathe now the final transformation this evening will kill you.'

'Then let it,' she spat.

He released her shackles and hauled her to her feet roughly.

'Let me go!' she cried.

He brought her close to him.

'Much as I would dearly enjoy watching your flesh dissolve in the new dilution,' he whispered, 'I am afraid the Doctor will not permit it. He wants you all ready by tonight.'

'Barbarian!' Rebecca hissed.

Mr Shottick scoffed. 'This from a bastard Jew? Get in!' he spat, then threw her into the pool.

As she splashed into the tonic-contaminated water she heard the other girls laughing. *Fools*, she thought. *Idiots*. Didn't they see that they were being tricked?

Her vision clouded over. Her lungs felt as though they were collapsing. Shottick stood over her like a demon amongst the angels peering down from the shadows high above. She'd kill him, she told herself, if it was the last thing she ever did.

Slowly she went under the water.

4.

Trudging up a deserted street inches deep in freezing snow Harish Patel struggled onwards, tired, cold and in serious pain with his shoulder. He checked his watch: almost four o clock. Four o' clock! He had been lost in town for hours. But now, he had lost sight of the Pavilion, and the black viaducts had wound their way out across the hills. Residential streets curving away from the town had brought him here, high on the hill overlooking the lights of town far below. He turned a corner and swore.

There it was: A dark but magnificent Art Nouveau cathedral emerging over the rooftops. A gloomy airship was suspended above it, almost lost in the shadowy clouds and straining against the hawsers which held it in place. Craning his neck upwards, Harish saw that wide aeroplane wings had been attached to the gondola, and that a high tower of scaffold soared upwards to meet it.

He ran to the park but a pair of swirling iron gates stopped him going any further. A sign announced:

THE QUEEN'S PARK SPA.
HOME OF DR. THEO'S EXCELLENT TONIC.
Closed to the Public.

Elated he climbed the gate and dropped to the snow on the other side, then ran for the trees, moving stealthily between them as the skies grew darker. The scaffold tower was between him and the spa, so he ran towards it across open ground.

Hearing voices, Harish quickly ducked into the scaffold, finding himself standing on a concrete platform at its centre. A line of people, each one carrying a wooden barrel, was moving towards the tower from the spa. He was surprised to see Mr Stanley leading them.

Harish climbed up into the scaffold, stepping across metal poles and one or two thick, black rubber pipes. A system of ropes and pulleys, weights and counterweights, running through the scaffold and the giant wings high above him tempted him to climb further when he heard voices from the procession of servants.

'You will begin loading the barrels with the lethal distillation,' Mr Stanley was saying to a huge, dark-skinned man. 'They must be attached to the explosive bolts on the wings -ten on each side.'

The man nodded. Harish climbed higher, his feet slipping on the black rubber pipes. A whip snapped the air like breaking ice and a voice shouted,

'Start filling from number three pipe. Now! Quickly!'

Something caught around Harish's foot and he slipped awkwardly, tumbling to the concrete. He bit his tongue to stop himself from crying out. Clumsy fool! He remained still, listening to his heart pounding in his ribcage. When he was sure that they had not heard him he disentangled himself and crept slowly to his feet. The rubber pipe supporting him had given way - one of five by the looks of it that were lying snaked across the ground. Three other pipes were already connected to three of five numbered brass standpipes. Two pipes were loose, one of these by his trip. But which one?

He picked up one of the pipes and connected it to one of the taps numbered three. It was an easy operation. He swung a brass wheel on the tap clockwise, and heard some kind of liquid sluicing through the pipe. As he was reconnecting the second pipe to tap number one, which proved to be more difficult, he heard a boy's voice, complaining,

'It's not working.'

Harish heard the slaver shout,

'Then go inside and switch on the tap, you bloody fool.'

Harish abandoned the half-connected pipe and climbed back up the scaffold. A moment later a boy, following the rubber pipe through his hands, reached the taps just as Harish's foot slipped on the scaffold, causing the metal to ring out like a bell. Startled, the boy looked up. Harish raised a shaking finger to his lips.

'Shhh,' he hissed. The boy looked over his shoulder, then back up at the intruder.

'Who are you?' he whispered. 'What are you doing here? Are you from the kitchens? I haven't seen you before.'

Harish climbed down.

'My name is Harish. I've got to get back inside or my master will go crazy.'

The boy nodded, understandingly, then walked behind the brass taps where three metal grilles were set into the concrete floor.

'You haven't been with us long,' he said, 'or you would know about this place. It's where we come for a smoke.' The boy pulled up the centre grille. 'Down there,' he ordered.

Harish stepped down, his feet finding purchase on a rusty ladder. Behind him Jhavesh closed the grille and whispered,

'I'll see you here again for a smoke, hey?' His grin flashed white above him, and then he was gone. Harish was not sure that this was such a good idea. *In fact*, he thought as he climbed further downwards, *I'd rather be stacking boxes of cornflakes than doing this.*

Sure, said the voice of his father, *give up, Hari, give up now. You always do when things get tough. That's why you will only ever be a shop boy working for my brother. And I expected so much more from you.* Perhaps he had let his father down, but he would never disappoint Rebecca.

His feet touched the ground. He was in a dark, vaulted chamber occupied by six, ghostly cylindrical tanks which Harish assumed fed the taps above ground. Fuel for the airship. Obviously.

Walking between the gurgling tanks, along an arcade of towering, highly-decorative arches, he stole a look at his watch and cursed. Nearly five o clock! Already?

Time was growing ever shorter.

As he made his way through the underground cavern he began to feel scared. The atmosphere was eerie, and peculiar noises made his heart beat faster. There must be rats down here, he told himself, and spiders and mice and - A low moan echoed around the shadowy walls. Half-formed figures peered out of the darkness at him: naked female torsos and mythical woodland creatures growing from the organic-looking piers. Their dead eyes seemed to track him.

Ghosts? His throat was dry. He pressed on, skipping quickly through the arcades. The moan came again, louder now. Which way should he go, he wondered, stepping backwards? The archways did not form corridors, not as such. Rather the underground space was divided by them. The whole place was a grim labyrinth of twists and turns and there was rubbish everywhere, filling up abandoned swimming pools that had been drained years ago.

Except for one.

The moan came again. Panicking, Harish turned, ran, then stumbled and fell headlong into a pool of salty water. Coughing and gasping he swam to the side, spitting the water from his mouth. He felt sick and his clothes were now soaked right through.

Walking away from the pool, dripping seawater, he moved through the arches at a run. Something reared up at him in the dark and he screamed. However, the shadow slipped to the floor and moaned. The scream stopped in his throat.

The shape was a man, Harish realised, bruised and bloodied, and close to death.

'Mr Baxter?' he whispered. The moan ceased. Baxter's watery eyes stared back at him through encrusted blood.

'Stop airship...' Baxter gasped. 'Stop them killing Baxter's people.'

Harish was touched by the pain in the man's voice.

'How?'

Baxter touched Harish's duffel coat, and lifted his wet finger to his lips. His eyes flashed at Harish.

'The sea,' he whispered, excitedly, 'take me to the sea...'

Harish shook his head, he did not understand.

'Water...' rasped Baxter, gripping Harish's wet coat. 'Need seawater!'

Now he understood.

'Come on,' said Harish, bending down and putting himself under Baxter's arm. He swore. Baxter was huge, impossible to lift with Harish's own shoulder still hurting badly. He tried again but it was no use. He set Baxter back on the floor, and massaged his shoulder.

'I can't,' he gasped. 'I can't do it. I'm sorry.'

Baxter looked up weakly at Harish.

'Need water, he whispered. 'Doctor hurt Baxter, Shottick hurt Baxter, then dump Baxter down here. Say, go find seawater before you die. It here somewhere. Then we come for you again. But if I find water ... Baxter get strong again, and go looking for them...'

'But I can't do it,' Harish answered. 'I can't lift you.'

'Then people die,' Baxter said sadly, and slumped to the floor.

Harish swore under his breath.

'Come on then, big man,' he said, and put himself under Baxter's arm again. Struggling, groaning, almost crying with the pain in his shoulder, Harish started to lift, to pull the man away from his incumbent position on the floor. He cried out, squeezed shut his eyes. He put his back into it, locked his legs together, pushed, roared, cried out against the pain in his shoulder, and heaved Baxter's dead weight off the floor in stages.

Step by step Harish dragged Baxter to the pool he had fallen in himself and then, when he was close enough, dropped him into it.

There was a splash. Baxter's body disappeared under the dark waters and Harish felt himself starting to panic. He had just thrown a dying man into a pool of water. Just then Baxter's head broke the surface quickly followed by the rest of his body. He was groggy as he climbed out of the pool, and there were scars across his face and chest that were starting to bleed again. But in himself, Baxter seemed stronger, rejuvenated by the salt water. Once on dry ground Baxter loped away from the pool at a run.

'Wait!' Harish cried.

Baxter stopped.

'I'm looking for a girl.'

'Plenty girl here,' said Baxter, pointing down a shadowy colonnade. 'That way.'

'Thank you.'

Baxter then ran away in the direction Harish had come from.

Harish, clutching his shoulder and blinking away the spots from his eyes, moved off into the passage and before too long came to a set of cobwebbed stairs spiralling upwards. He followed them up and at last emerged into the spa proper. *Almost there*, he breathed. *Almost there*.

5.

Rebecca tossed her bronze tresses away from her face and inspected her neck in the leaf-patterned mirror. Two patches of silvery skin reflected the low light of their room. Mary Jane was sitting on a bunk with her hands between her knees.

'Rebecca,' she said quietly.

Rebecca touched her new gills. They hadn't opened yet, perhaps because she hadn't spent as much time in the water as the others had.

'Rebecca, I'm scared!'

Rebecca stopped looking at herself. She stood and walked over to the bunk, putting her arm around Mary Jane's shoulders.

'Don't worry,' she whispered tenderly. 'I'll find us a way out of here, I promise.'

A thunderous knocking disturbed their quiet. Mary Jane jumped and a voice in the corridor outside barked,

'Two minutes.'

'Rebecca?' hissed Mary Jane.

'Sssh.'

Two minutes later the door opened and the girls were taken from their room.

6.

Harish dragged his water-soaked body through dimly-lit corridors similar to those he had been in downstairs without a clue as to where he was going. He found his way into a pool room, but nobody was here and the pool had been drained. Moving away into another room entirely, which turned out to be a gallery overlooking a much bigger pool, he was surprised when someone grabbed hold of both his shoulders and threw him bodily across the wood-backed chairs. Getting ready to defend himself, Harish bunched up his fists.

'Hey hey!' A toothy grin lit up in the dark.

Harish stopped in mid punch.

'You?'

'The name's Jhavesh. Sorry, man, I thought you was after me.'

'Why should I be after you?'

'Cos I ran, and they're looking for me. I shouldn't be here, but they're curing my girl-friend tonight.'

'What's wrong with her?'

'She's been changed.'

'Changed?'

'The Doctor's a beachcomber,' Jhavesh explained grimly. 'He kidnaps girls who drift in from other places and brings them here for experiments. He tried it on me, look.' Lifting up his fingers Harish saw that they were joined by thin skin membranes. They were webbed. He shivered, his teeth chattering.

Jhavesh led Harish to a railing on the edge of the balcony overlooking the huge, blue-lit pool below.

'He's trying out the different effects of his Excellent Tonic on the human form. It went wrong a couple of weeks ago, and the girls started to turn into fish. This pool is filled with a distillation of Tonic balanced to cancel out the effects of the previous experiment. Those barrels we loaded onto the airship, you remember?'

'Sort of.'

'They're loaded up with a more lethal distillation. It's too scary, my friend,' Jhavesh said bitterly. 'Once she's been healed I'm taking Mary Jane away from here. Brighton has many beaches, I know a place where-'

A light came on and Mr Shottick entered the room from below. The two boys ducked behind the rails and watched as ten girls wearing colourful saris filed in, herded by a trio of muscular servants. Among the girls - Harish's eyes widened. Was it her? Really? Yes, yes it was.

'Rebecca,' he breathed.

7

'You'll all be pleased to know,' said Mr Shottick to the girls, 'that the Doctor has perfected his latest transforming dilution.' He smiled and gestured at pool behind them. 'It's in here. When you jump in you should all be returned to normal.'

'Liar!' spat Rebecca.

Mr Shottick smiled and walked towards her.

'Perhaps you should go first.'

Rebecca stepped backwards, feeling the edge of the pool at her heel. He reached out a hand ...And pushed Mary Jane into the pool. She fell backwards with a scream and a splash. Mr Shottick grabbed Rebecca by the shoulders and spun her round to face the girl struggling in the pool.

'Push them in!' he yelled. 'All of them!'

The musclemen stepped forward, advancing on the girls, but Mr Shottick held Rebecca, his lips touching her left earlobe.

'I want you to watch what happens first,' he whispered, 'as each of your friends is transformed cell by cell.'

'Why are you doing this?' Rebecca hissed. 'It's inhuman.'

'When the sea-dwellers are destroyed by the Doctor's lethal Tonic we'll need people to harvest the Well. The transformation will enable you all to survive underwater.'

'What if we refuse? You can change our bodies but not our minds.'

Shottick laughed.

'Oh, you won't refuse. If you do not return to the Well every few days, then you will die.'

Rebecca stared, horrified, as the girls thrashed in the water. The room was filled with their screams. It certainly was not curing them.

'You next,' hissed Mr Shottick, and shoved Rebecca into the pool.

'Rebecca!' screamed Harish, leaping over the gallery and sliding down a metallic pier.

Jhavesh, frozen by fear until now, ran after him, screaming his hatred of Mr Shottick.

Tricked, they had all been tricked! Harish crashed to the floor, knocking his bad shoulder in the process, and then ran at the pool.

Two muscle-bound servants stood in front of him while Rebecca went under the water.

'Get out of my way!' he cried, lashing out with his fists.

'You again!' exclaimed Mr Shottick. 'Hold him!' They caught Harish and lifted him off his feet.

'Get off me!' he yelled, struggling. 'Rebecca!'

'You're too late, boy!' laughed Shottick.

Rebecca's head came up and Harish saw with horror that a pair of gills now flared on her neck like bony wings. Stunned, he saw that she was swimming for the edge of the pool where Mr Shottick stood. He saw her grab the thin man's ankle, and watched as she pulled with all her strength. Mr Shottick dropped and was pulled screaming by the girls, into the pool, clawing uselessly at the slippery tiles with his hooked fingers.

'Help me! Help!'

Under he went.

Jhavesh arrived and cried out for Mary Jane, his voice full of pain. The musclemen relaxed their grip and Harish shrugged himself free. He ran and fell to his belly at the water's edge where he reached into the pool with his left arm. He caught something and hauled upwards, feeling the pain in his bad shoulder as he produced Mr Shottick's dissolving head and shoulders.

'Aagh!' he dropped the head. Rebecca rose to the surface some way along, coughing and choking.

'H - Hari,' she coughed. 'Wh -where the hell did you come from?'

Harish scrambled towards her and helped her out. As soon as she was up on the poolside, the sari clinging to her body, he hugged her and pressed himself against her soaking flesh. He couldn't believe that he had found her at last. Jhavesh meanwhile stared at Mary Jane in fascination, who tread water at the far side of the pool, beckoning to him. He muttered a prayer, then jumped into the pool and swam after her.

'Jhavesh, no!'

Rebecca held Harish back as Jhavesh went under then emerged thrashing in pain.

Harish's head reeled. He slipped to the floor, feeling numb, shivering.

'What the hell is going on here?'

'Come on, lover boy. It isn't over yet.' Rebecca hauled him to his feet with a clammy hand. 'We've got to stop Doctor Theo dropping his tonic into the sea and killing thousands of people.'

Harish stole a last look at Jhavesh clawing at his face in the reddened pool before Rebecca dragged him out through the door and into another of the spa's numerous corridors. Mary Jane was screaming.

'I thought the Tonic was supposed to provide everlasting youth and vigour!' he cried, his voice hoarse, his teeth still chattering. His soaked pants were beginning to chafe.

'It does,' answered Rebecca. 'In small quantities. It comes from a Well under the sea, and the marketed stuff is one part wellwater to about a million of seawater and natural minerals. There's a race of people who live by the Well, they've been there ever since their part of Brighton collapsed into the sea half a century ago. They used to let the Doctor harvest the Well for his tonic but recently they've stopped him having access to it. I think Baxter had something to do with that. Now the Doctor plans to kill them all by dropping a stronger distillation into the sea. The Well will be his alone, and he'll use us to harvest it instead of the sea-people.'

Harish pieced together the few shreds of information he had.

'Jhavesh told me the barrels on the airship were loaded up with tonic.'

'So that's how he plans to do it.'

'But if the tonic is made from Wellwater,' said Harish, 'how would that kill the people who live there?'

'It's a delicate environment. Too much Wellwater to seawater will kill them. If someone put too much carbon dioxide into the air you'd die wouldn't you?'

'I suppose so.'

'Well there you are then. We have to stop him.'

8.

Doctor Theo was bad. Baxter had always known that, and after many years had managed to convince his people of that. The Doctor just wanted to make money, sell his so-called Excellent Tonic, become a millionaire, have lots of power. But Baxter was going to terminate his delusions of grandeur, and more importantly he intended to stop the Doctor killing the people he loved.

So now he was climbing up the scaffold tower to the airship. Hand over broken, bloodied hand, bringing his heavy feet up one rung at a time. Up he climbed, up into the cold, howling wind, until at last he reached the top of the tower. Once there he ran, stumbling along the wooden boards forming the platform roof, across to the rope ladder which led up to the winged gondola straining against its metal hawsers .

Behind him there was a crunch of machinery. A bell chimed and the elevator doors opened.

'That's far enough.'

Baxter, one hand on the ladder, looked around in the buffeting wind.

'Stanley,' he grunted, letting go of the rope.

Mr Stanley was holding a gun at him, a silver, multi-barrelled revolver with little green lights on the chamber that winked in sequence.

'Stay where you are, Baxter. I don't want to hurt you.'

Baxter moved round, keeping his eye on Mr Stanley.

'Doctor kill them all,' he shouted at the wind.

'I know.'

'Got to stop him, Stanley.' Baxter moved forward.

There was a boom, the world exploded, and Baxter felt something ripping through his guts, an intense pain. Mr Stanley ... had ... had shot him ...

Baxter lunged forward and knocked the hot gun from Mr Stanley's hand.

'We used ... to be friends!' he roared. Mr Stanley looked horrified. Baxter grabbed hold of Mr Stanley's shoulders and squeezed, hard. 'We used to be friends...' he hissed.

Slowly Mr Stanley started to scream. Baxter crushed him, squeezing as hard as he could until the bones cracked. Mr Stanley squealed like a pig, but the noise meant little to Baxter. He threw the weak creature over the edge of the scaffold and then headed up into the gondola via the swaying rope ladder, trying to ignore the vicious shoots of pain flowering through his flesh.

Baxter climbed up into the door, slipped on the threshold, rolled into the darkened gondola, and then stood carefully. His head felt light, buoyant. It was as though he was in the water again, free, swimming away from all the pain in the world, safe in the womb of the sea.

But he was dying, he knew it. He heaved himself forward through the green-hued darkness, holding onto the golden walls for support. He had to drop the barrels here, where they would smash open on the ground and leak away harmlessly into the snow. His watery gaze swept the ghostly dials, levers and switches on the wood and brass console facing him. So many. He blinked rapidly, washing his eyesight clean for one final moment of clarity, it was all he needed.

Yes. There it was!

Baxter reached out for the lever that would fire the explosive bolts holding the barrels of deadly tonic on the wings.

A brief moment of hesitation.

He could feel ... something: A prickle of fear on the back of his scaly neck... Baxter turned slowly and saw the Doctor sitting in his glass and brass jar, saw the slanting red eyes staring at him through the bubbling, thick, green liquid.

The terrible, hypnotic voice that came from the very air itself was full of hatred:

'Baxter, I command you -'

But not this time. Smiling, Baxter pulled the lever down as he slid to the floor, his freed mind swimming away into the Sea of Forever.

9.

Harish followed Rebecca blindly as they charged through a door into a grand, ornate reception area, with desks, sofas and potted plants standing on a lush carpet. A row of circular windows looked outside onto the scaffold tower and the winged airship.

'Now what?' said Harish, feeling the need for some dry clothes more than anything.

He let Rebecca pull him behind the big reception desk towards a side door that perhaps would lead outside.

There was a flash of light, an explosion.

The windows burst apart, spraying glass into the reception area and both Harish and Rebecca screamed, diving under the big desk in front of them and covering their heads.

More explosions. An endless percussion. A frightening drum roll of successive, thunderous detonations, and a howling, screaming gale of heat ripping through the air.

They stayed there for a long time, sitting out the waves of heat and final tinkling of glass, waiting until the aftershock of the explosion had died down and their ears had stopped ringing. Finally they both raised their heads and looked out through a massive hole in the

outside wall onto a rippling curtain of fire rising into the night.
'The airship,' whispered Harish.
'Like the Hindenberg,' muttered Rebecca, standing.
They walked carefully through the destroyed wall, and stared at the flaming tower of scaffold and the balloon of fire that had collapsed on top of it. They could feel the heat even from here as parts of the airship's skeleton broke and fell away from the infernal mass.
'Fuel,' said a watery voice behind them. Jhavesh and Mary Jane stood there. Harish tried not to look too closely at the changes in their faces.
'The tonic for the barrels was stored in tank three,' said Jhavesh. 'You switched the pipes so we loaded from tank one - which contained fuel for the airship. Well done.'
Rebecca squeezed and kissed him.
'My hero,' she whispered, with only a touch of mockery in her tone.
'My shoulder,' said Harish. Rebecca pulled her arm away.
'Is something wrong with it?'
Harish frowned.
'No,' he said quietly. Then he remembered that it had been in the water briefly when he had lifted Mr Shottick's head out of the pool. So the tonic really did restore health and vigour. *But at what cost*, he thought, looking at Rebecca who, although not quite as far gone as the others, still had a silvery sheen to her skin, a quickness in her eyes and, of course, the gills on her throat.
Something nagged at him. He looked at his watch. 'Quarter past seven,' he said tiredly, then looked at Rebecca. She was gorgeous in the firelight.
'Our ride home leaves in fifteen minutes.'
She stared back at him.
'Let's go then.'
'Do you know the way to the marina?'
'Of course I do!' she replied.
Harish grabbed her hand and pulled her away. They ran, shouting their goodbyes behind them and headed into the streets of Brighton running as fast as their wet clothes and fatigue would allow. They made it, just in time.
Captain Bain's boat was growing foggy and indistinct as Rebecca and Harish pounded down the quayside, running as fast they could to reach it before it vanished entirely. The Captain and Poltice helped them onboard.
'Glad you could make it,' he said.
'So are we,' coughed Harish, shivering.
'There's a small problem,' the Captain informed them.
'Oh?'
'Stormy seas ahead. We might not make it back to your own world, at least not to-night.'
'We'll take the chance,' said Rebecca, gasping for breath and putting her arm around Harish.
'Then get inside and buckle up,' said Captain Bain. 'It's gonna be a rough ride!'

Paul Laville

10.

Three iron fire engines descended with a howl on Queens Park spraying water from the hoses attached in loops to their scorched, red-painted hulls. They hovered like metal balloons over the blaze while below them a crowd was gathering to watch the spectacle.

All eyes were on the fire, so no one saw the shrivelled black thing which scuttled lizard-like away from the flames and dropped down a grate in the ground. No one saw the forked tail flipping over in defiance as it slipped away and vanished into the subterranean darkness beneath the frosted streets of Brighton. No one knew of its anger, or of its desire to return.

Yes, it would return, and next time there would be no mistakes.

This story was sponsored by Scheherazade Magazine

12 Bolinbroke Avenue

Peter James

It was a pleasant looking mock Tudor semi, with a cherry tree in the front garden and a wooden birdbath. There was nothing immediately evident about the property to suggest a reason for the terror Susan Miller felt each time she saw it.

Number 12. White letters on the oak door. A brass knocker. She began to walk up the path, drawn by an invisible magnet whose forces she was powerless to resist. Her terror deepening, she reached forward and rang the bell.

'Susan! Susan, darling! It's OK. It's OK!'

The dull rasp faded in her ears; her eyes sprang open; she gulped down air, staring out into the darkness of the bedroom.

'I'm sorry,' she whispered, hoarsely. 'The dream. I had the dream.'

Tom settled back down with a grunt of disapproval and was asleep again in moments. Susan lay awake, listening to the steady, endless roar of the traffic on the M6 pouring past Birmingham, fear swirling like icy water through her.

She got out of bed and walked over to the window, afraid to go back to sleep. Easing back the edge of a curtain, she stared out into the night; the large illuminated letters advertising IKEA dominated the horizon.

The dream was getting more frequent. The first time had been on Christmas Eve some ten years back, and for a long while it had recurred only very occasionally. Now it was happening every few weeks.

After a short while, exhaustion and the cold of the late October air lured her back into bed, and she snuggled up against Tom's unyielding body and closed her eyes, knowing the second nightmare which always followed was yet to come, and that she was powerless to resist it.

Christmas Eve. Susan arrived home laden with last minute shopping, including a few silly gifts for Tom to try to make him smile; he rarely smiled these days. His car was in the drive, but when she called out he did not respond. Puzzled, she went upstairs, calling his name again. Then she opened the bedroom door.

As she did so, she heard the creak of springs and the rustle of sheets. Two naked figures writhing on the bed swirled in unison towards her. Their shocked faces stared at her as if she was an intruder, had no right to be there. Strangers. A woman with long brown hair and a grey-haired man. Both of them total strangers making love in her bed, in her bedroom. In her house.

But instead of confronting them, she backed away, confused, feeling as if it was herself who was the intruder. 'I'm sorry,' she said. 'I'm so sorry. I'm - '

Then she woke up.

Tom stirred, grunted, then slept on.

Susan lay still. God it was so vivid this time, it seemed to be getting more and more vivid just recently. She had read about dreams in women's magazines, and she tried to think what this dream might be telling her.

Confusion was the theme. She was getting confused easily, these days, particularly over time. Often she'd be on the verge of starting some job around the house, then remember that she had already done it; or rushing out to the shops to buy something she had already just bought. Stress. She had read about the effects of stress, and that it could cause all kinds of confusion and tricks of the mind.

And she knew the source of the stress, also.

Mandy. The new secretary at the Walsall branch of the Allied Chester & North East Building society, where Tom was deputy manager. Tom had told her about Mandy's arrival a year ago, and had then never mentioned her since. But she had watched them talking at the annual Christmas party last year, to which spouses and partners were invited. They had talked a damned sight too much for Susan's liking.

She had not been sure what to do. At thirty-two she had kept her figure through careful eating and regular aerobics, and still looked good. She took care over her short brown hair, over her make up and her clothes. There wasn't much else she could do, and confronting Tom without any evidence would have made her look foolish. Besides, she was under doctor's orders to stay calm. She had given up work in order to relax and improve her chances of conceiving the child they had been trying for for five years. She had to stay calm.

Unexpectedly, the solution presented itself when Tom arrived home that evening.

'Promotion?' she said, her eyes alight with excitement.

'Yup! You are now looking at the second youngest ever Branch Manager for the Allied Chester & North East Building society! But,' he added hesitantly, 'It's going to mean moving.'

'Moving? I don't mind at all, darling!' *Anywhere*, she thought. *The further the better. Get him away from that bloody Mandy!* 'Where to?'

'Brighton.'

She could scarcely believe her luck. In their teens, Tom had taken her for a weekend to Brighton; it was the first time they had been away together; the bed in the boarding house had creaked like mad, and some old bat in the room below had hollered at them and they'd had to stuff sheets into their mouths to silence their laughter.

'We're going to live in Brighton?'

'That's right!'

She flung her arms around him. 'When? How soon?'

'They want me to take over the branch at the start of the New Year. So we have to find a house pretty smartly.'

Susan did a quick calculation. It was now mid November. 'We'll never find somewhere and get moved in within a month. We've got to sell this place, we've got to...'

'The Society will help. They're relocating us, all expenses paid, and we get a lump sum allowance for more expensive housing in the South. They're giving me the week off next week so we can go there and look around. I've told the relocations officer our budget and she's contacting some local estate agents for us. '

The first particulars arrived two days later in a thick envelope. Susan opened it in the kitchen and pulled out the contents, whilst Tom was gulping down his breakfast. There were about fifteen houses, mostly too expensive. She discarded several, then read the details of one that was well within their range, a very ugly box of a house with a small but charming garden, close to the sea. She liked the idea of living close to the sea, but not the house. Still, she thought. You spend most of your time indoors, not looking at the exterior, so she put it aside as a possible and turned to the next.

As she saw the picture, she froze. Couldn't be, she thought, bringing it closer to her eyes. Could not possibly be. She stared hard, struggling to control her shaking hands, at a mock Tudor semi identical to the one she always saw in her dream. Coincidence, she thought, feeling a tightening knot in her throat. Coincidence. Has to be. There are thousands of houses that look like this.

12, Bolinbroke Avenue.

Number 12, she knew, was the number on the door in her dream.

Maybe she had seen the house when they had been to Brighton previously. How long ago was that? Fourteen years? But even if she had seen it before, why should it have stuck in her mind?

'Anything of interest?' Tom said, reaching out and turning the particulars of the modern box round to read them. Then he pulled the details of the semi out of her hands, rather roughly. 'This looks nice,' he said. 'In our bracket. In need of some modernisation. That's estate agent-speak for a near wreck. Means if we do it up it could be worth a lot more.'

Susan agreed that they should see the house. She had to see it to satisfy herself that it was not the one in the dream, but she did not tell Tom that; he had little sympathy for her dreams.

The estate agent drove them himself. He wore a sharp suit, white socks and smelled of hair cream. 'Great position,' he said. 'One of the most sought-after residential areas of Hove. And it's a bargain for this area. A bit of work and you could increase the value a lot.' He turned into Bolinbroke Avenue, and pointed with his finger. 'There we are.'

Susan bit her lip as they pulled up outside Number 12. Her mouth was dry and she was shaking badly. Terror was gripping her; the same terror she previously experienced only in her dreams gripped her like a claw.

The only thing that was different was the *For Sale* board outside. She could see the cherry tree; the wooden bird bath. There was no doubt in her mind; absolutely no doubt at all.

She climbed out of the car as if she were back in her dream, and led the way up the path. Exactly as she always did in her dream she reached out her hand and rang the bell.

After a few moments the door was opened by a woman in her forties, with long brown hair. She had a pleasant, open natured smile at first, but when she saw Susan, all the colour drained from her face. She looked as if she had been struck with a sledgehammer.

Susan was staring back at her in amazement. There was no mistaking, absolutely no mistaking at all.

'Oh my God,' she said, the words blurting out. 'You're the woman I keep seeing in my dream.'

'And you,' she replied, barely able to get the words out, 'Y- you - you are the ghost that's been haunting our bedroom for the past ten years.'

Susan stood, helpless, waves of fear rippling her skin. 'Ghost?' she said finally.

'You look like our ghost; you just look so incredibly like her.' She hesitated. 'Who are you? How can I help you?'

'We've come to see around the house.'

'See around the house?' she sounded astonished.

'The estate agent - made an appointment.' Susan turned to look at him for confirmation, but could not see him or Tom - or the car.

'There must be a mistake,' the woman said. 'This house is not on the market.'

Susan looked round again, disoriented. Where were they? Where the hell had they gone?

'Please,' she said. 'This ghost I resemble - who - who is - was - she?'

'I don't know; neither of us do. But about ten years ago some building society manager bought this house when it was a wreck, murdered his wife on Christmas Eve and moved his mistress in. He renovated the house, and cemented his wife into the basement. The mistress finally cracked after a couple of years and went to the police. That's all I know.'

'What - what happened to them?

The woman was staring oddly at her, as if he was trying to see her but no longer could. Susan felt swirling cold air engulfing her. She turned, bewildered. Where the hell was Tom? The estate agent? Then she saw that the *For Sale* board had gone from the garden.

She was alone, on the step, facing the closed front door.

Number 12. She stared at the white plastic letters; the brass knocker. Then, as if drawn by a magnet, she felt herself being pulled forward, felt herself gliding in through the solid oak of the door.

I'll wake up in a moment, she thought. *I'll wake up. I always do.* Except she knew, this time, it was different; and that she never would.

This story was sponsored by Stuart Grey of Austin Grey Estate Agents

Message in a Bottle

Elizabeth Counihan

To: Mr Tom Hobb
Pooks Barn
Rothermead, Sussex

From: Mr J Teazle
Teazle & Rickard,
Private Investigators
Brighton, Sussex

1 April 2000

Dear Mr. Hobb,
As per our telephone conversation I am sending the following items together with a summary of our report:

1. *A letter addressed to yourself and signed by 'Lorelei Hobb'.*
2. *Pages from a diary in the same hand with entries covering dates in May 1997.*
3. *Printed brochure entitled 'Seven Hills Artists 1997' in the manner of a Brighton Festival brochure.*
4. *A glass bottle in which the above items were contained.*

* * * * *

Darling Tom,
I do not know if this letter will ever reach you. Robin has promised to deliver it. I know that you are the only person in the world who would believe I was not insane. Even Donal, much as I love him, would send for the shrinks...but lovers are not like twins, are they?

I am writing this letter in May - I think it is still May. Julie wanted me to do a piece on the Festival for her arty web site, that's what finally persuaded me to come here. You wouldn't believe I nearly turned her offer down on account of that old phobia you and I had about going to Brighton; do you remember? That's how they trapped me - the phobia wasn't so silly after all.

It all started quite normally. I arrived at the station. The crowds were in holiday mood, some in fancy dress - because of the Festival I suppose. A band was playing 'Sussex By The Sea'. I was jostled by people speaking in French, Portuguese - you name it. It was all so good-humoured. I felt hot and sweaty but relaxed. Then floating high up like a lark I heard the forlorn sound of pan pipes above all the noise and bustle.

I pushed through the crowds and hesitated at the exit, looking for the taxi rank. The pipe-player was sitting on the pavement just outside the archway - a curly-haired young beggar. He lowered the pipe and dislodged a black cat from a pile of magazines beside him. *'Big Issue*, ' Miss?' he said.

I asked him to play again. He took up the pipes and played *Greensleeves*, prettily enough but without the melancholy of the tune I had first heard. He took my £1 coin and handed me the magazine and with it a coloured brochure. I tried to give it back but he grinned and said,

'It's part of the Festival. Go on, you'll enjoy it.' As I walked off I heard the pipe start a jig tune and out of the corner of my eye I glimpsed the cat gambolling about on two legs. Quite a show.

I glanced at the leaflet in the taxi queue. 'Brighton Festival Umbrella Events - Seven Hills Artists' it read. I flicked through the pages. They described a variety of art exhibitions showing at private houses and other sites, open only at weekends during the Festival. On the last page was a map of the town and information for visitors. Then, at the bottom, in smaller print: *Seven Hills Artists would like to thank Goodfellow's Travel for providing free transport between venues. Visitors wishing to avail themselves of this facility should commence their tour from venue no.1 at the West Hill location.* I looked at the map. Venue no.1 was right here, under the station itself.

Maybe I could have escaped then, but I remembered how Julie always raves about the fringe events at Edinburgh, so I thought it would be just her kind of thing. That's when I got out my diary to make some notes. I've ripped out the pages for you, Tom. You can see I have headed each section with one of the locations listed in the brochure. I was just making notes at first, then trying to hold onto my mind.

Tom, I can hardly bear to say this. I think we may never see each other again. I think everything has changed. Perhaps you wouldn't even know me if we did meet.

Tell Donal I love him.

Lorelei

* * * * *

1) The Pink Underground, West Hill: furnishings, ceramics, glassware.

Hilariously weird! All the icons - posters of Gone With the Wind and The Wizard of Oz inside what must have been a station underpass. Background music from *Casablanca.* And I had the charming host all to myself - he has a wicked grin, tattooed arms and wears a feather boa. I was the first visitor of the morning. He seemed to recognise me from somewhere - friend of Julie's? He produced some very salty biscuits and two glasses of champagne, insisting we drink 'To the future and past of Brighton.'

The exhibits include a huge pink bath, a cocktail bar decorated with seagulls in neon lighting and an array of beautiful Art Deco-style glasses. I'm strongly tempted to come back and buy a set before I leave Brighton.

When I was ready to leave Titty (he calls himself that), led me through a bead curtain at the back, down a short tunnel and, still below ground, onto a miniature railway platform giving onto a single track. There's even a little waiting room with old railway posters inside, and flowers in hanging baskets outside. There was no one but me and Titty. I saw a signal light change and a little electric train, very smart in yellow and brown, rattled in. And now I'm sitting all alone in a carriage got up like a Victorian drawing room, elegant brocade sofas, even a chandelier. There's a musty smell. How come this place exists and isn't full of little boys and their dads? As I write this we are burrowing through the chalk hills on our way to the next exhibition. I can't wait.

2) The Hoggy, Carlton Hill: jewellery, lace, objets trouvés, objets volés etc.

I found this exhibit almost too realistic, almost scary. The exit from the underground railway was up a narrow spiral stairway of rusting ironwork. It seemed far from safe and there was no information to indicate that the venue was unsuitable for children or the disabled. I found myself emerging from a manhole in the middle of a very narrow, cobbled street. Not an attendant in sight. There was a dirty wooden sign pointing to 'The Hoggy' which is a pub, the tallest building in a street of terraced, squint-eyed houses, many of them boarded up. It was oppressive. I had thought all these slum houses were knocked down years ago, but evidently not in this town.

I climbed a few dirty steps up to the 'open house', or rather open pub. It's like something out of a Hammer Horror film - creaking inn-sign, sinister-looking locals gathered around the bar and so on; very well done and probably authentic, but it was rather over the top seeing I was the only visitor (as far as I could tell). A strong smell of fish inside and out, but that has to be for real surely. I couldn't quite decide what was part of the exhibition.

There didn't seem to be a lot for sale, unless you count the strangely dressed, fish-smelling inhabitant who asked me, in a fake yokel accent, to buy some lace, of all things. He turned quite threatening when I laughed. I think he said, 'You owe it to us after what you did,' but I must have misheard.

Fortunately a curly-haired lad sitting at the bar told the man to 'Leave the young lady be. She means no harm.' That shut him up all right, but by then I felt uncomfortable and only had a quick look round the old pub. It has certainly been restored to an incredibly authentic-looking condition of antique squalor and would be well worth a second visit, preferably with a group of friends.

I looked around for signs or instructions about the next venue but there was nothing. I hesitated to ask the youngster although he appeared genuinely friendly. He got up from the bar-stool and said 'I'll show 'e the way, Miss.' He must have been part of the act, with the same Mummerset accent as the older man so I was happy to go with him.

We went back to the manhole in the street. The smell of fish was worse than ever. And then I heard loud squealing followed by the sound of a cat growling over its prey. Perhaps a taped sound effect, but I don't really think so.

I scuttled down the iron stairway and back onto the platform, followed by the young gypsy. I saw now how dirty the station was here, all blackened as if an old steam train habitually used it. And I hadn't noticed before that it was lit by gaslights. I kept looking around for rats. Thank goodness I didn't have to wait longer than five minutes for the train - electric like the first one, but this has dingier rolling stock. The boy waved politely and said 'See you soon!' - forgetting ye olde accent for a moment.

I think I must be sitting in one of the original 'third class' coaches. Wooden seats and zero suspension - not too easy to write legibly. Next stop Round Hill.

3) Gypsy Eva's Tent, Round Hill: Performing arts, incense, crystals, mandala. Have your fortune told!

Something is happening to me. I must try to write coherently.

We were back on the surface but I had not seen where we had emerged. I am certain I was riding on an electric train when I boarded at Carlton Hill, but at some point it had been exchanged for a steam engine, now pouring smoke and whistling away in answer to a fairground organ. We were in the middle of a fun fair, which I could see occupied a large, grassy area at the top of the hill. I could not see any houses but I think they must be further down, the roofline blocked by caravans, stalls and fairground equipment. The track waved erratically, passing several booths and tents, most fronted by a barker. We passed a bowling alley, a helter-skelter and a darkened tent full of flashing, beeping video games. The engine stopped, with my carriage drawing up directly outside a striped awning, with a bead curtain hiding the interior. Above was a crudely drawn picture of a gypsy fortune-teller. I got out.

There were plenty of other people around this time, but everyone I saw was in some kind of fancy dress. Some wore clothes that could have come straight out of a tv production of Jane Austen. Some had gypsy outfits or costumes from the old-time Harlequinades and Punch and Judy shows. Many were masked. Otherwise it seemed like any other fair - plenty of stalls selling candy floss and ice cream, a smell of hot sausages and bacon; a big wheel and numerous carousels all playing different tunes with numbers of children and little dogs adding to the noise.

I pushed through the bead curtain and entered Gypsy Eva's tent. The beads were edged in little bells that jangled as I crossed the threshold. The uproar outside ceased instantly as if I had stepped into a soundproofed room. I blinked in the gloom. There was a scent of sandalwood. As my eyes adjusted I saw Eva herself, picked out from the darkness by a pearly light. She wore a long, brightly coloured dress, jet beads and matching earrings. She could have come from a New Age shop - maybe she did. I wanted to look at the exhibits, not that I could see much, but she insisted on telling my fortune or 'fate', as she called it, so I gave her 50p and sat down at her table. Something in the lighting made her face appear to float disembodied, her eyes upturned and white. As she bent over my hand heavy, fringed eyelids flicked like a camera shutter and then I saw her pupils dilate.

'So, at last, Robin has found you,' she murmured. Her hand flicked, removing the drape from an object on the table beside her - and this was really odd - what lay beneath was not a crystal but a computer screen! She studied it for a long time.

'Well, what's my fortune?'

'Your fate was set by others many aeons ago. A wrong was done. And now you have eaten our bread and salt.'

'What's that supposed to mean?'

Her eyes blinked twice, slow as a cat's.

She said, 'Although the child is blameless, we have never forgotten the crimes of its forbears. Forward is back.'

I thought the woman must be mentally disturbed, so I got up quickly and turned back towards the opening in the tent, but the lighting had dimmed suddenly and I could not find the way out.

Then I felt a cool breeze and saw daylight coming in through a narrow opening on the other side of the tent. I pushed my way outside.

It's quite cold out here and the light is wrong. Everything is wrong. I couldn't hear the fair and when I went around to the other side of Eva's tent there was nothing - no steam organs, no carousels, no people. Only a cornfield.

Did I pass out? No. I can't have. Not for long enough for them to have taken the fair down. It's still only midday. No, that can't be right, my watch battery must be running out. I refuse to be spooked by all this. I'm going back inside the tent.

Later: Eva's tent is empty. There is dust inside. No chair, table, computer. Just one of the Festival brochures pinned to the canvas wall. What is going on?

I don't feel too good. I'm sitting down opposite the cornfield. I can see a crop circle, no; it's a maze. I always thought corn came later in the year. Maybe it's some other crop...not a soul in sight.

I can see something moving in the middle of the maze. I'm going to check it out.

4) The Gatehouse, Hollingbury Hill: See the iron-age fort as living history.

I feel like I'm trapped in this wilderness, wherever I am. I'm frightened now and I don't think there's a way back. I was still kidding myself that it was all a show. But it isn't. I saw a man killed.

I went through the corn maze, following the movement at its centre. The corn was too high for me to see over and by then I felt quite scared, half-expecting to bump into the Minotaur. But there in the middle, all by itself, was a horse - a small, white horse with gilded reins, attached to a painted, glittering cart. No driver. The horse made a gentle whickering sound. I remembered about the free transport between the exhibitions. I forced myself to believe I was still in the natural, real world so I climbed onto the cart. The horse started off – why did it make no sound? All I heard was a faint singing in the air but even sitting up on the cart I still could not see above the corn. There were birds high up between white clouds, but the singing was human, I think. The little cart rocked up and down. We went round the maze like a ride on a merry-go-round. Am I drugged? Something in Titty's champagne? There must be a reason for this.

When we emerged I was in a strange country and there were no houses – none in any direction. A cold wind blew. Then I saw the hill and the fort.

The ground rushed under us - I didn't know horses could run so fast. He jumped over a huge ditch and floated over an embankment. We pulled up before a massive wooden palisade, so high I had to crane my neck to see the spikes at the top. A scrap of coloured paper fluttered in the crack between two of the posts adjacent to a vast gate.

I jumped down from the cart and reached for the paper. It was one of the brochures. The wind nearly ripped it from me but I clung onto it as if it was a lifeline to the real world. I turned back towards the horse and cart but they were gone. I was in a desolate landscape of rough grass and hillocks. Far away to the south I saw a grey and white glitter - the sea, and on it some dark shapes, boats I think, and just inland tiny darts of flame But I saw no birds, no living creature in any direction. Grey clouds poured across the sky. A gust of sea-wind brought the smell of smoke. Nearly weeping, I banged on the gate.

'Help!' I cried, 'Help!' Rain pricked my bare arms.

The massive structure swung open. Immediately I heard the sounds of human activity, men shouting, horses neighing, the clatter of metal on metal. A young man stood at the threshold, smiling.

'Come in quickly,' he said, 'You are the last.' I slipped inside and the great gate closed again.

I asked, idiotically, 'Where am I?' and he told me in a matter-of-fact tone that we were in the Iron Age hill fort of Hollingbury. I dared not follow up with the question *when am I.* The answer was all around, flickering in and out of my vision, like - yes, say it - like ghosts. A kind of corral holding sheep, and odd-looking cattle. Another for horses. Several round, wooden houses. I heard women calling in an unknown tongue and little children ran inside the huts. I saw some, others I only heard, although I knew they passed near to me in the teeming rain.

I heard a man cry out from somewhere above me, and looking up, I saw a tall wooden structure rather like a pylon, set on the apex of the hill. The lookout was shouting and gesticulating from the top. I heard men cursing, although the words they used were unknown to me. There were shadows running to the palisade. Some I saw clearly - warriors with spears and axes, others were only half-visible, rippling as if at the bottom of a pool, but their metal weapons gleamed in the dull light. I smelled wood smoke and damp greenery and manure.

The young man was still beside me. He wore yellow oilskins, his curly hair had unravelled in the rain and he stood apart with folded arms.

'You know, don't you. What's going on? Help me for God's sake!'

'Living history. Didn't you read the leaflet?' His voice was gentle but there was something faintly malicious in his smile. 'Perhaps you should go inside,' he added. 'It's rather wet and not very safe out here.' I scurried past him and the gates swung to behind me.

A shower of burning missiles flew over the palisade, one or two striking the roofs of the dwellings but the rain extinguished them immediately. The young man bowed slightly and flapped a wet hand in the direction of the central hut. More burning objects landed near us. I coughed as the smoke caught at my lungs. Now I heard terrible howls and whoops from outside the palisade. The warriors inside responded with screeches of defiance. Still grinning, the young man gestured again and I ran for the building, pushing through the animal hide obscuring the doorway.

It was dark inside. The place smelled of straw and urine and smoke. I heard children crying. The women were keening. After a while I saw the gleam of eyes. But in this place I was the ghost. I am sure they were not aware of me. The cries outside increased. I heard scuffling and children protesting. I think the frantic women were dragging their children towards them in a last instinctive effort to save them.

Shouting and the clash of weapons at the doorway. The hide curtain wrenched aside and the light instantly blocked by a man's body that crashed to the ground.

I could not see the blood but I could smell it. The man groaned and his breath bubbled. More men sprang across the threshold. I felt women push past me, screaming imprecations.

The intruder fell but two more dark shapes forced their way in.

A small body pressed against me and I felt a child's hand clutch at my trouser leg just below the knee. In the dim light I could barely make out the toddler's upturned face but her wailing voice cried 'Ma-Ma' in the universal language. This was no act but a real child in terror, a child who was able to perceive me. At the same moment a great hand reached for her - one of the invaders. His other hand held a knife.

My reaction was instinctive. I snatched her, thrusting her behind me and away from her would-be murderer. I saw his glittering eyes and I knew he saw me. My arm was grabbed and I was dragged into the rain. A dark, bearded man grinned into my face as he held me at arm's length. His forehead was painted like a football fan's but he wore animal skins. I felt his hands dig into my flesh. As I struggled, the body of a man was tossed out of the hut, followed by a woman who threw herself, weeping, onto his corpse. She was dragged off by one of the invaders.

My captor gripped both my hands in one fist and flourished his knife with the other. He stank of sweat and dirty leather. He looked at me with some curiosity and started to pick at my tee shirt with his knife.

Further from me the fight was only half-real. A solid-looking defender had his throat cut by an insubstantial dagger wielded by a translucent hand. Again I could smell the blood. I gagged and slipped in the mud, my arms wrenching as the bearded man tightened his grip. A cool voice spoke next to me.

'Mmm. Interesting. So you at least of your accursed tribe are willing to help one not of your blood. Seen enough? I think it's time to get on to the next exhibit, don't you?'

I knew who it was all right. I yelled 'Get me out of here, you bastard.' He just murmured 'Okay, keep your hair on,' I tried to twist round but I couldn't see him.

It got darker. I thought it was a thundercloud. I heard gasps from the men about me. Blackbeard let go of me and pointed towards the sky. My eyes followed the direction of his pointing finger. Something was descending onto us, blotting out the light. Where its hooves landed the mud dried in plumes of steam. The rain hissed on its white, gleaming flanks. This was no toy fairground horse but a huge stallion from heaven or hell or some even more mysterious world. It snorted and turned towards Blackbeard, snapping at his fingers. He screamed, clutching a bloody hand.

'Well, get on him. I've decided to give you another chance,' said the cool, invisible voice. I jumped. There was no saddle or stirrups or anything to hold onto. But I was on his back clinging to his mane. Sparks flew from him and I felt the tingle of electricity stinging my hands.

As he leapt into the sky I heard a loud clap of thunder and in the flash accompanying it I saw, from far above, the fort with its central hut on fire despite the rain. The smell of burning wool or hair reached me. I heard faint laughter following us.

It was now entirely dark except for the white gleam of my steed but the clouds jumped out in shades of red, purple and silver in the lightning flashes. The noise terrified me. I felt I must be insane. I still think this must be the explanation.

I am in a worse place now, where the Horse let me down. There is a terrible smell. This must be the end of the world, or the beginning of it. I am cold. I can hear owls. The sky is not quite black now. I think the moon is rising.

5) Whitehawk Hill: the day-to-day life of Neolithic man.

I am writing this by the light on my key ring

This is another hill, the one where they hold horse races in the Brighton I came from. Is this past, present or neither? But is there room in either world for demon horses, for puppet masters called Robin who sell *The Big Issue* in seaside towns and cast spells on unwary passers-by? And why me? What did he mean about 'another chance?'

The sky is dark except on my right where there is a patch of misty silver. There is enough light for me to see that the hills below me are snow-covered. It was May when I left my world. The air is still, but there is a vile stink of rotting meat. I can hear a low-pitched buzzing some way to my left. It is getting louder.

A dark procession is approaching. They carry no lights so I cannot distinguish them. Now I hear a croaking sound coming from higher up the hill.

The sky is getting brighter. I see that I am standing about fifty metres from a circular bank and there is another inside it higher up the hill. There are several dark platforms near the centre. Crows are pecking at what lies on them and I think they are the source of the stench. I cannot see what lies dead there and I don't want to.

The people are closer. I think they are men except for the one in front. They have very white faces like clowns. They are carrying a moaning figure. The one in front - the woman - stops beside a gap in the first embankment. The rest go inside. Why can I still see them when I am out here? They are still humming or chanting. They are going round and spiralling inward - like I did in the corn maze. I feel that I am with them, that the woman who leads them has my face. I am screeching and jumping up and down, ululating, waving a stick - no a thigh bone with bits of string hanging from it - or are they strips of flesh?

I can see the victim. He has dark, curly hair and little horns.

6) Coney Hill:

I think I'm still alive. I'm writing this, so I must be.

We dragged the horned boy to the centre of the Hill along a series of ditches. The shadowy structures I had seen were like huge wooden tables. They put dead people on them for the crows to pick. I don't know how they died and then I didn't care. There were two big stones in the middle, one flat, one upright with a hole in it. The flat stone was bloodstained. The men formed a circle. They put the boy-creature on the stone and the witch-woman who was me sprang into the circle, faced the moon and stretched out her arms, wailing and screaming. The men hummed and shouted louder than ever. The moon rose, growing larger. Its weight oppressed me. I knew that when its rays touched the boy we would kill him as we kill all unhumans, with a starstone knife, whose slightest touch is deadly to them. She/I raised the jagged knife. It scattered the moonlight onto him like silver dust. He screamed in a human voice. The people cheered.

I remembered the words: *So you at least of your accursed tribe are willing to help one not of your blood.* And in that moment I became wholly myself.

I threw the knife away.

The boy tumbled from the stone and skidded down the slope, his feet crackling in the hard snow. A huge black shape leaped over the embankment. He scrambled onto its back and gestured obscenely at us, crowing like a cock. I felt the growl of the great cat through the soles of my feet and saw the flash of its amber eyes. Then both disappeared into a patch of shadow.

I felt myself seized and flung onto the icy ground. Everything went black until I awoke to a chorus of crows and gulls. The tribesmen had tethered me, unconscious but alive, to one of their burial platforms. The stench choked me and I vomited, disturbing three crows that had settled on my body. I screamed and tried to move my arms but could not. I watched the dawn break, waiting for them to return for my eyes. I saw gulls wheeling in the brightening sky.

A crow descended towards me. The dawn light flooded over it, turning it gold and then white. It plunged downwards, growing ever larger. I shut my eyes as its great beak skimmed over me. I felt my bonds snap and I was lifted up in huge claws. My eyes stung in the sudden cold and I opened them. I saw the clouds floating far below, shadowing a forested land lapped by a grey ocean. I shivered, but the bird held me against its warm breast. It had soft, warm fur, more like a cat than a bird. But I could not breathe.

I woke up here in the sunlight. I think it is May again. I am lying in a meadow of grass, daisies, buttercups, poppies, clover and lots of other flowers that look vaguely familiar but whose names I don't know. I am not sneezing. There are rabbits jumping about all over the place. Also bees and butterflies. And deer. I can hear music.

I have no idea where Coney Hill is but I don't think this can be Brighton.

I have just looked up at the top of the hill. A young man with curly hair is playing the pipes. There is a black puma curled at his feet. The young man has little horns.

7) Black Rock:

That's where I will be going Tom and I don't suppose I will come back again. Robin says I won't want to. Robin is very old and has several names. He knows a lot. He has explained that what I did today, or thousands of years ago, set right an ancient wrong that my people – our ancestors, Tom – did to his. So things will be different in my own time now. Brighton, England, the whole world could be changed by what I did.

I can see all the way down to the sea now. A river runs all the way from here. Robin will ask a sea creature to fetch me when I am ready. Blackmalkin, his familiar, does not like water.

Black rock is far out to sea. I can hear the mermaids plucking on fish-bone harps. The sea is dashing against their rock. They are laughing at the drowning sailors.

And now I must leave. The biggest of all creatures is sailing upriver towards me, spouting on her way.

Summary:

The glass bottle (also enclosed) had been carefully sealed against contamination by seawater. It was handed into a police station on January 1st AD 2000, by a local vagrant who had been sleeping rough under the pier and claimed that he had found the bottle washed up on the beach. The police have not found evidence of criminal activity and no person of the name 'Lorelei Hobb' is listed as missing. No further police action is forthcoming.

As you are aware, there was some delay in the authorities forwarding the enclosures to you as the address given by 'Lorelei Hobb' was of a non-existent street in Crawley which, as you may know, is a small village on the Sussex/Surrey border.

Following your instructions to investigate further we discovered the following facts.
1.There are no records at Somerset House of a 'Lorelei Hobb' born in this country during the past century.

2. Examination of the bottle by experts has failed to ascertain its origin. The glass is similar to that commonly used for bottling soft drinks but the brand, 'Dr. Theo's Excellent Tonic', is not recorded. The glass shows evidence of sustained damage compatible with a history of prolonged exposure to the sea. The paper used for the letter, diary and brochure are of unknown manufacture.

3. The printer and publisher of the brochure entitled 'Seven Hills Artists' are not listed and no such group as 'Seven Hills Artists' has exhibited at the Brighton Festival Fringe.

4. There are many factual errors in the written text, the most glaring of which is, clearly, the reference to a racecourse at the site of Britain's most famous Ancient Monument at Whitehawk Henge.

We sympathise with your anxiety to ensure that the author of the written enclosures is not a 'missing' sister, but we respectfully suggest that they are the work of an elaborate and shameless hoaxer and we strongly advise that further investigation is unlikely to prove fruitful.

Be assured that Teazle and Rickard will continue to investigate any possible leads but, once again, we would respectfully remind you that no evidence has been forthcoming to date of the existence of a previously unrecognised member of your immediate family.

Yours faithfully,

J.J.Teazle

Insinuations

Deirdre Counihan

'You bloody cow, Gwen! Can't you even get your sodding arse out of The Land of Nod for long enough to see me to the door?'

Gwen grappled her way up to the surface, gradually realising that the slimy green weed of the Mere-Queen's lake was only really her sweat-soaked sheets and that the bursts of primal thunder cast after her by her would-be captor had, in fact, been nothing more than the sounds of her sister Igraine descending the stairs with attention-seeking switched up to maximum.

Gwen took a deep breath and blinked herself back to reality. She must not mind. She must not mind that the whole world seemed to be going to Hove in a handcart - no, that wasn't right - but nothing had been going right for her since the cliff fell down.

'When you had to do this,' Igraine ranted on to an unresponding world, 'I carried your stuff down the road for you, you bitch!' Needless thump of overnight bag (which Gwen had distinct recollections of packing for her at some time in the small hours). 'Yes, I know I did! AND I put a bar of my organic chocolate into your pocket - almost a new one. But you - you're quite happy to snore away like a sow and let me go to my fate without so much as a crumb of breakfast!' Igraine paused in her flow of invective just in case Gwen showed any signs of rising to the bait. 'Oh well, dream on then. See you on Wednesday - If I haven't slit my wrists before then!' she yelled by way of final riposte as she let the door slam.

Gwen listened for the possible sound of tinkling glass from its stained glass window and, reassured, groped for her slippers. She reached the window of their parents' room just in time to see the last of Igraine's spare black figure, her mane of long, dark hair billowing out behind her, as she rounded the corner at the brow of the hill.

'A retreating figure!' she mused. How would Igraine adapt to going on retreat? More pertinently, perhaps, how would the holy nuns at the Pastoral Centre cope with Igraine and her friends enduring a time of enforced meditation? Gwen had quite enjoyed it herself, a couple of years back now, when her year group had been herded through this initiation rite, but then solitude and introspection had always been her thing, rather than Igraine's, which, in the present circumstances, was just as well.

She stumbled her way back through her parents' pristine bedroom, tightening the sash of her white towelling robe as she did so. Had they been back at all? She hadn't heard them. Downstairs her mother's neat post-it note on the fridge informed her that they must have been.

'See you on Wednesday. Perhaps the workmen on the cliff would appreciate a cup of coffee?'

No one had fed the cats. Was her mother's underlying message a suggestion that she got properly dressed at some time in the next couple of days? Probably. Talk about laying it on thick and thin: between them, Igraine and their mother seemed to be incapable of finding the right line to take.

The whole family was sincerely concerned by Gwen's sudden dive into inexplicable debility at such a crucial point in her education, but no one seemed to know quite how to handle it. As test after test revealed nothing of any medical significance, no one was crass enough to doubt her genuine suffering, but their initial bewilderment was now starting to take on a slight hint of impatience. Gwen reflected that in a more enlightened age the whole thing would have been put down to a simple bewitching. The mummified corpse of some small furry animal suitably impregnated with a vile-smelling unguent would be popped under her pillow, or rammed down her bra, and no more would be said.

Their father, ever wise, in fact never said anything about her health at all. Gwen found this to be an oasis of calm in the storm of Igraine's honest invective and their mother's earnest questioning. Dad did seem grateful that someone was taking the trouble to keep the house nice for once. When both of the girls had been going to school, and both their parents at work in town, the place had been perfectly tidy, but no one had time to consider things like fresh flowers in the sitting room, or deodorant blocks in the loo.

In those pre-post-it-note days, people could, and did, write the family messages in the thick dust - but it had been ordinary household dust then - not a soul destroying thin layer of concrete like it was now.

Gwen went back to her room and tried to decide what to wear. Even simple decisions like this were exhausting at the moment. Who would ever know or care whether her panties matched her bra or toned with her T-shirt? - but the effort of trying to locate everything brought her out in a cold sweat. Decency at last achieved, she let the green roller blind whang up to reveal the new day and the stunning view from the back windows.

LANCE had been at work in the night!

Before her, on the other side of the glittering rail-tracks, stretched the rolling hills of Brighton bathed in the morning sun: rows of pastel-painted houses, waves of ocean-grey roof tops stretching from the shimmering line of the sea on her right to the softly green and golden downland on her left with its distant pair of white windmills that fronted the long smudge of the grey stone walls that safely cradled the town. And there in the middle of it someone called LANCE had done his worst (again).

None of the inhabitants of Hillcrest had been too happy when, twenty years or so ago, well before Gwen and Igraine's time anyway, the-powers-that-be had allowed the demolition of several of the attractive Edwardian family villas that fronted the river walkway deep in the valley below them. These had been replaced by a collection of substantial office blocks, small enough to get round the planning regulations, but exactly large enough to deprive Hillcrest of its view of the burbling Wellesbourne and the rose gardens of Preston Park.

Everyone in Hillcrest knew that they would fail as a venture; there simply wasn't the trade in that part of town to fill them. The Hillcresters were obliged to look down helplessly from their vantage point on the ridge while the buildings below them went slowly to seed. The windows became broken, a noisy congregation of mixed bird life moved in, and, worst of all, its site, directly on the main road and rail link from London, meant that the town's graffiti fraternity decided to designate it the numero-uno location for showing off their daring and expertise.

The most intrepid, and, it had to be admitted, talented, of their number was someone who went by the tag of 'LANCE'. LANCE could be found everywhere, writ large all the way up the motorway, and yet writ small in every public loo, both Gents and Ladies. Today Gwen was confronted by Lance's tag written new and neat in blue and silver on every single unbroken window in the deserted office block immediately on the other side of the railway cutting, smack in the middle of her morning view.

Gwen pulled her hair back into a ponytail and took a deep, fairly dust-free, breath. She drew back the bolts on the kitchen door and set off down the garden to speak to the men on the cliff - she had noticed from her bedroom window that there were two of them today, an oldish one called George who was quite often working there and a younger one that she hadn't seen before. The lawn crunched beneath her feet, completely coated with concrete. Everything in the garden was covered in a thin film of liver-grey dust, most of the plants were dying and the cats had become so disorientated that they no longer saw any point in burying their shit and in consequence it was most important to tread with care.

When she and Igraine had first entered the garden as toddlers it had been a paradise of roses, perched out on the cliff top like a magic carpet. They had rolled all over the sun-dappled grass like mad things. 'We have got to live here, Mum!' they had said, and had all lived there happily ever after.

Then one morning, more than a year ago now, they met Gwen's putative boyfriend, and classmate, Bruno, wheeling his bike up the hill at the crossing by the railway bridge. Instead of his usual early morning raptures as to what LANCE had created to improve the neighbourhood overnight, he observed rather worriedly: 'I think you ought to look at the bottom of your garden, girls. All those saplings and bushes seem to have gone somewhere.'

Understatement! By the time they all got home from school the railway company had loaded the entire mini woodland onto trucks and spirited it off. The whole chalk cliff had broken away at the footing of their eastern garden wall, like the dotted line in a bit of loo paper - there was nothing but an unsupported waist high wall between them and a hundred-foot drop down onto the railway track.

When the family and their immediate neighbours made frantic enquiries as to what the railway company, who had owned the missing land beyond the walling, proposed to do about ensuring that the cliff would be properly shored up and their properties protected, they were horrified to discover, that since the railway cutting had been dug by act of parliament in the first place, they were not owed any right of support by the railway company at all. In fact, they were told, in no uncertain terms, that if anything, like an intrepid child, for instance, were to fall from their property onto the railway line below, they, and not the rail people would be liable for the damage.

And so the great war of nerves began. The inhabitants of upper Hillcrest were a determined bunch, and very inventive. The end result was a climb-down by the Railway, who, though never actually admitting that they might have some responsibilities to the residents of the ridge above them, none the less agreed to spray the cliff fronts with liquid concrete in a new and experimental process if the families would stop making them look so mean and stupid to the rest of the British public.

After hacking off any loose chalk that was still clinging to the cliff face, the contractors started on the spraying. Two powerful jets, one of water and the other of cement dust, met each other at high velocity close to the cliff face, with the end result that all the gardens at the top end of Hillcrest were bathed in a perpetual cloud of light grey dust. Having fought so hard for something to be done, no one was going to lose face by complaining. It was, quite literally, a matter of gritting one's teeth and bearing it. But it had been a nightmare for them all, particularly Gwen, who was in the middle of exam work. There was nowhere that she could breathe easily. When she left her bedroom net-curtains to soak in detergent and ended up with half a bucket of concrete, she gave in and bought the roller blind.

But today the workmen seemed to be engaged in some exciting new part of the process involving huge sheets of thick black polythene. Gwen looked over the wall and saw it stretching in vast billows right down the cliff.

'Hello, 'Rapunzel!' How are you feeling today?' said George, looking up at Gwen from the precariously-sited work platform. 'That bugger 'Lance' must have had a busy night last night from the look of it, mustn't he?' He nodded in the direction of the vandalised office block on the other side of the rail-track.

'Yeah, but that's nothing; have you seen what he's done under the roof of the New England Road Bridge?' observed his young companion. 'You'd think he must be able to fly, some of the places he gets to.'

'My Mother wondered if you would both like a cup of coffee or something?'

'Thanks; very considerate woman, your Mum. 'Rapunzel's' Mum is on T.V, Wayne.'

'Anyone I'd know?'

'How do I know what you'd know? How late do you watch? She's on late, isn't she, 'Rapunzel'? 'The Caring Man's Cracker' they call her, don't they - if you don't mind my saying so?'

'No, not at all.' Gwen was rather proud of her Mum, in fact. 'Yes she's on very late these days. She does The Crux Of The Question.'

'What, HER? Well, bugger me!' From his tone, Gwen gathered that Wayne didn't exactly class himself as a caring guy. 'But your name's never really Rapunzel? That would be a bit cruel.' Nor did he feel the need to be too tact-aware either!

'Well, it's Gwenevere, actually, I'm afraid. Tea or coffee?'

'O.K. - 'Rapunzel' it is! Strong tea and don't hold back on the sugar, thanks.'

What a spotty little whelk! Back in the kitchen Gwen looked around for a mug unpleasant enough to sum up her estimation of him - she usually tried to match the mug to the man. She always gave George a friendly looking mug with the Tetley Tea Folk on it. At the very back of the cupboard she struck gold with an ex-Easter-egg number featuring a pastel teddy bear in green pyjamas.

'You were on T.V. too, weren't you? I remember,' said Wayne, gulping down his tea and not even noticing the revolting bear, let alone catching on to her private joke about a green (k)night. 'Something to do with shoring up this cliff. I thought you hadn't got a cat's chance in hell of getting anything done - but there you go!'

'Well, I was only on the Southern TV channels - and the local lot - nothing special'. Gwen shivered slightly in the morning breeze and tried to forget the crestfallen look on Igraine's face when it had been Gwen who got interviewed because it had been at a time when Igraine had been down at school. So unfair, because it had been Igraine who had done all the real leg work in their cliff-campaign. She had only been able to cope with the phone and the post herself - oh, and painting the big banner of sheets that they had strung down the cliffs so that their message was clearly visible from all the trains on the London line. That had been great fun, before she got really ill.

'Looks like the wind's picking up a bit,' she observed as she took back the empty mugs. 'Will it muck up what you are doing with that plastic?' She remembered the struggle that the cross winds had made for them when they were hanging the painted sheeting. It had taken four of them: her, Igraine, the ever hopeful Bruno, and one of Igraine's friends, Alph - who had finally hit on the notion of employing some of the bricks from around the barbecue as weights, several of which they lost in the cutting. Looking down into the cutting, she noticed a whole section of some newspaper bowling along as a live thing, a large red three clearly visible at its hub, while it cartwheeled its way along the railway track for all the world like a ball of tumbleweed in a cowboy movie.

'Not a problem.' George reassured her. 'Wayne knows what he's doing - don't you, boy?'

Two and a half days on her own! All the things she could do! She could really get down to her Art exam project without interruption - even start to think about her potential Art College folio. She could play the sort of music that she liked without Igraine being so scathing about her taste that she gave up and switched the TV back on. Her brain started to simmer with all sorts of ideas for her preparation work; she completed sheets and sheets of studies in her mind's eye. Regaining the kitchen, she put on her tape of Fidelio full blast and started to tackle the Monday morning chores with a will.

As was her habit these days, she dropped off to sleep after lunch, lulled by what was now a romantically wuthering wind. She did not wake up at teatime, because there was no Igraine to come slamming back into the house. When she did come to, she found herself in total, sucking, almost breathing, darkness. Somewhere, she was sure, she could even hear the neighing of a horse.

Gwen had to take a great deal of care about checking on reality. She appreciated that from a very early age she must have gone in for waking from one dream into another. She had still never got over the chilling fear, one moonlit night, of watching a group of silvery men, all pastel shades of the rainbow, climbing silently around in the pear tree outside her window.

She felt for the lamp behind the sofa, the sitting room, in all its normality, clicked into view. The weird, wuthering and sucking noises continued, however, and there was that neighing sound again! One got all sorts of strange noises wafting up from the engine sheds in the rail cutting but she had never heard anything like that before.

Was she dreaming? She did the obvious thing and switched on the TV - perfectly normal late evening News. She switched channels to be ready to watch her mum, gave herself a bit of a shake to restore normality, and headed for the kitchen to catch up on tea and supper, almost convincing herself that the continual slurping and flapping noises from outside were not all that unusual.

Someone was banging on the back door. Gwen froze, butter knife in hand - there was no real access to the back door, apart from the neighbours' garden walls - or the cliff. Then she heard the horse again. It sounded as though it was right outside the kitchen window, breathing through the circular ventilator that was set into the glass.

Clearly, this had got to be a dream! Gwen pulled up the Venetian blind onto the night. The window pane was fogged by clouds of steam pouring from the nostrils of a huge silver-grey horse. The horse had wings. When the pounding on the door started again, Gwen decided to open up.

The horse's owner looked rather like the Silver Surfer, but he had long, curved eyes of a tantalising blue.

'Anything I can do to help?' asked Gwen.

'The darkness has enveloped us! We cannot escape!'

'Wow' said Gwen, looking out at the undulating roof of black. 'The plastic from the cliff must have been blown right over the house - so that's what that funny sucking noise was. I wonder if we can even get out at the front?'

'My horse and I are thirsty from the dust,' said the figment of her imagination (or what ever he was). 'And I have trodden on something unpleasant on your lawn.'

'Oh dear, do take an antiseptic wipe. Would you like a cup of tea? I've just made it. Do you mind Earl Grey?' Some instinct made her reach for Igraine's 'Silver Alien' mug that had been sent off for from the Fortean Times. 'And a bucket of water for your horse? There is that nice transparenty-blue one by the loo door - see?'

As he turned to manoeuvre his amazing mode of transport into the scullery (so much easier to shift than her bike, she noted, since it was prepared to help you) she glimpsed a ripple of gold from a star on his silvery shoulder. Was it his skin or some sort of jump suit? The huge horse fitted itself in neatly between the fridge and the sink and folded back its head to preen like a swan.

'Very fragrant,' observed the silver man, cradling the teacup in both hands as he sat beside her at the kitchen table.

'Would you mind very much if I watched my mother's show on T.V.? She hates it if we miss it.' Gwen had no intention of letting her mother down - even in fantasy.

'I saw you on TV,' mused the silver man. 'From my home in the clouds. I thought you the most perfect of Earth's women.'

Igraine arrived home on the Tuesday evening, rather than the Wednesday (having singularly failed to benefit from introspection) and found the roof of their house, and the one next door, aswarm with young men in bright orange jackets who were trying to detach the rogue polythene from the chimney stacks.

'Are you okay? Gwen? - You look sort of dreamy,' she said with real concern. 'It must have scared the daylights out of you to find yourself in a huge plastic shroud like that. Have you got in touch with Mum or Dad? Would you like me to ring the doctor? I'm amazed it didn't take out the T.V. aerials though! Oh for fuck's sake, what have you done to my

Fortean Times mug? It's all sort of melted round the rim this side. Did you leave it on the stove or something?'

Surprisingly few months later, Gwenevere pushed her 'miracle baby', Fidelio, up New England Hill while his Aunty Igraine hovered in attendance, laden down with paper nappies.

'No, I'm not going to let you hang anything more on the pram handles, Gwen. The weight would just do you in all over again. I know everyone's saying that it was just the 'pregnancy-denial' that was making you feel so grim, but I think you ought to watch it. Honestly I do. Couldn't you let Bruno take a bit more of the load, too? He would love to really. I think you are just being paranoid. Males should be held answerable for the consequences of their actions!'

'And pigs might fly!' retorted Gwen, glancing lovingly up to where 'LANCE' was emblazoned high above them on the roof of the railway arch.

Prince of Lamentations

Liz Williams

Why hurry to break a man's heart? Jack O'Hanlon thought, as he headed towards the Pier. Twilight came early on these November evenings and there was a drift of rain coming in from the Channel: grey air, a dark heaving sea, and a black bloody mood to match it all, Jack thought. He jammed his precarious trilby more firmly upon his head, thrust his hands deeper into the pockets of his overcoat, and stared morosely at the blurred lights of the Pier. At least they'd finally got around to repairing the bomb damage from the war, not before time... This was a dreadful night, the sort of weather when anything might be abroad; the kind of night that conjured up uneasy thoughts of the sidhe or the huldra. Moreover Jack was now both cold and wet, but either seemed preferable, at the moment, to going home or back to the cramped office of the studios and telephoning Goldstein. He had rehearsed the conversation over and over again: none of the variations sounded any better than the first, and he couldn't hope to pull the wool over Goldstein's eyes. Uneasy thoughts circled around in his mind like a reel played over and over again: without Velma Merlin, there would be no movie, and without a movie, the studio would have to close. He could probably find work as a director somewhere else, perhaps in one of the little studios starting up in that American place - Hollywood, was it? - but it wouldn't be the same as Brighton.

'Can't we find someone else?' Dolly had asked, when Velma's agent had called with the bad news, and for the first time in the six years that they had been working together, Jack had lost his temper, shouting

'Who the hell else is there? Who? Who?' on a rising note like a crazed owl. Velma had been their last shot, and now that she had summarily deserted the rainy lights of the south coast for the brighter illuminations of the South of France, Dolphin Studios could not afford anyone else.

Conscience and reluctance to fact facts underwent a brief conflict within Jack's psyche, and he began walking back the way he had come. He owed it to Goldstein to break the news personally, however hard it might be. Halfway along the Esplanade, however, the gale swept in with a scouring blast of rain. Jack's hat was snatched from his head and whirled up into the wind. Abandoning any hope of retrieving it, he ran for shelter beneath the arches of the Esplanade. To his surprise, the amusement arcade was still open, and its glittering promise of light and warmth drew him within.

Once inside, he found himself facing a row of Victorian penny-in-the-slot machines. For the first time that day, Jack smiled, thinking that the ornate cabinets were, in a way, the origins of his own industry. The last cabinet, half hidden behind a pillar, was different. It hosted a plaster gypsy: her mouth fixed in perpetual grimace and her crimson dress shadowed by dust. The words 'Madame Devi' were inscribed in faded gilt across the top of the cabinet. Jack wondered how long she had been sitting there, motionless. Moved by a sudden sentimental pity, and ignoring the bored, scornful stare of the boy in the booth, he fished in his pocket for a penny and inserted it into the slot. Whorls and spirals and leaves decorated the machine, and when Jack touched it, a thick layer of dust adhered to his fingers.

Slowly, the gypsy creaked into life. Jerkily, she selected a card from the pack on the table and pushed it in his direction. Jack had once had a girlfriend who read the Tarot and he knew the suits: Transformations; Intentions; Lamentations; Ancients. The card that now lay before him was one of the suit cards: a young man with a dark and glittering smile, riding a tiger. *The Prince of Lamentations. Too bloody right,* thought Jack. *That would be me.* Glancing up, he felt as though someone had punched him in the stomach. The plaster face of the gypsy remained locked in its rictus smile, but the eyes were golden and alive and suffering. With a movement that seemed full of effort, a rigid finger shoved the card a fraction further along the cloth, and the living eyes pleaded: *help me*. But Jack began to back away, out through the shadows of the amusement arcade and into the rain, and the last thing he heard was the whirring of the mechanism as it wound down.

Opening his front door, Jack stepped inside and switched on the lamp. Rain poured down the single tall window and he caught a glimpse of his own face, haloed with wet light, blurred as if by tears. He dropped his sopping overcoat in the bathtub and sat heavily down by the phone. Taking a deep, slow breath to still the fluttering in his stomach, he picked up the receiver. As he dialled, he prayed a cowardly prayer: that Goldstein would still be in London, deep in some Soho pub, chatting up Tennant or MacLaren Ross or that drunk Welsh poet friend of his and trying to wring a half decent script out of someone. *Be in London, Harry. Be anywhere but at home, waiting by the phone.* Goldstein picked up the receiver on the first ring.

'Yes? What?'

'Harry, it's me.' Even that sounded doom-laden, Jack thought. 'Look, we need to talk.'

'Velma's pulled out,' Goldstein said, bleakly. 'I spoke to Dolly. Thanks for trying to spare my feelings, Jack. I'll see if I can try to talk the backers round, but...' Jack had never heard him sound so old.

'I'm sorry, Harry,' he said.

'It's not your fault,' Goldstein said wearily. 'I'll call you tomorrow.' And he hung up.

Jack sat silently for a moment. Goldstein's despair echoed in the vaults of his head; the plaster gypsy's golden eyes still pleaded. Jack cracked a bottle of scotch, kept under the sink for medicinal purposes, and took a long, spluttering drink. Half an hour later, the bottle was half empty. Goldstein and the gypsy rotated in his head like figures on a merry go round. *Prince of Lamentations*. If he couldn't help Goldstein or himself, Jack thought with laboriously drunken logic, maybe he could help Madame Devi.

'What the hell,' said Jack, and went to find his second best overcoat.

The lights were on in the Royal Pavilion, glowing through the rain like the ghost of Christmas. Jack paused before heading around the side to the gateway. Feeling at once foolish and nervous, he tried to remember the ritual precautions, drilled into him at school like every other Brightonian child. It had been a long time since Jack had thought about such things. Carefully, he walked three times around the free-standing gate, then through it backwards. As he took a careful reversed step through the gateway, he felt a vertiginous tilt as though a lift was descending. The rain stopped. Jack blinked. The grounds of the Pavilion swam with underwater light. Mist wreathed the trees and the lights of the town were no longer visible. Glancing up, however, Jack found that he could see the stars: clear and burning across the sky, in constellations that he did not know and which seemed to shift and change as he watched. He shivered, though the air around him was mild, and turned to face the Pavilion. The building seemed smaller than in his own world; its angles subtly redefined. Its domes were lit by a faint golden glow, but one thing remained the same. The lights were on.

Trying not to hold his breath, Jack walked to the main entrance. Here, perched on a ledge, sat a small silver bell. The place was eerily quiet. Jack paused for a moment, then tentatively picked up the bell and rang it. Echoes sang through the still air. The panelled doors of the Pavilion swung open.

Jack waited, but no-one appeared. He took a cautious step forward, and peered around the open door. He could see a long hallway; mirrors reflecting into infinity. As in the Pavilion in his own world, a series of Chinese figurines stood at intervals along the hall. As Jack watched, their heads swung round to stare at him.

'Good evening?' Jack called.

'Well,' a voice said tartly. 'This is a surprise.'

Startled, Jack looked up. The woman was reclining on the ceiling, her shadowy muslin skirts trailing through the air. The high white crown of her hair glistened with diamonds; her eyes were as pale as glass. She stretched out her arms and arched her back. He caught the sharp glitter of her smile.

'Someone's come to see us...' the woman murmured. 'How nice...'

'Madam? I'm looking for the Prince. I wondered if it might be possible to, um...'

The apparition's slippered feet floated down until they were level with his eyes. She began to descend, jerkily, striking a series of mannered poses as she did so. Jack waited. At last the sidhe's feet touched the crimson carpet. She gave him an imperious hand to kiss; her skin was bitter cold against his own. He performed the greeting with as much speed as decency allowed and she gave him a slow sidelong smile that spread across her face like ice over the surface of a pond. Surreptitiously, Jack licked frost from his lips.

'Come with me,' she whispered, adding 'Keep close, won't you? It's so cold...'

She took him companionably by the arm. By the time they reached the dining hall, Jack's teeth were chattering.

'Come through,' the sidhe instructed. She led him through the dining hall, which seemed thronged with people: beautiful, shimmering in the cascading light, skin as golden as sunlight and as cold as the moon, but when he turned to look at them, there was no longer anyone there. Above him, the little dragons which thronged the chandelier twisted around its central chain and dropped their bronze heads to stare at him. He could see a fire deep in their eyes, like the crimson flicker at the heart of old wine.

'Don't mind them,' the sidhe said. She nestled close and cold, and led him through a mirrored door into a long parlour. Someone was lying on a chaise longue in the shape of an Egyptian barge, before a seawood fire.

'Prince?' the sidhe whispered. Jack held his breath. The figure's head turned to look at him. The Prince was hard to see. Jack had the impression of a dark face, midnight eyed and marble hard. Silky black hair fell across the Prince's shoulders, and Jack remembered the whispered stories of the Pavilion's lord. *Not from these parts*, people would murmur. *Not one of the sidhe, the Old People. They say the Prince comes from the East.*

'Highness?' Jack forced himself to say.

In a voice that seemed to come from a very great distance, the Prince said:

'A visitor. Aha.'

Something rustled at the side of the chaise longue: a pointed face swam out of the air and blinked leaf green eyes, then disappeared. The Prince smiled, engagingly.

'It's been such a long time since anyone came to see us...' His hand caressed a shimmering mass of hair, coiling out of nothing beneath his fingers. 'Anyone human, that is. We thought you'd forgotten all about us...'

'Everyone holds you in the greatest respect -'Jack started to say. The Prince's smile widened.

'So they should. So tell me, to what do we owe this particular honour?'

'Well,' Jack said, trying to focus on the matter in hand. His companion was leaching heat from him; he could feel his fingers growing blue and wrinkled inside his pockets. The Prince sighed.

'Please...' He made a little flicking motion with one languid hand and Jack tried not to stare as the sidhe woman swarmed back up the wall. He could feel her gazing down at him as she hovered over his head; he did not dare look up.

'Mmm?' the Prince said. Jack hastily told him of the encounter in the amusement arcade, addressing the air shortly in front of the Prince's feet. He risked a quick glance and saw that the lambent gaze was riveted upon him. It was hard to look into the Prince's eyes. Jack swallowed.

'But how *interesting*.' The Prince said. 'I was in danger of becoming bored for a moment, but now...Well.' He uncoiled fluidly from the couch and took Jack's arm in his own, then began walking down the room. He smelt of sandalwood, Jack noted irrelevantly, and a dry, bitter fragrance like ash. Heat seeped through Jack's sleeve into his skin; he felt as though he were melting.

'But my dear fellow, of course we'll help you in assisting this damsel in distress...' the Prince was saying. 'I mean, really...an amusement arcade. How tragically quaint. Come with me.'

Jack allowed himself to be taken down the corridor. As they walked, he could hear music from the room ahead, but when they stepped through the door there was no-one to be seen. A faint note lingered on the air, and then was gone. Up in the decorated dome of the music room, two more dragons snapped and spat; a shower of fiery sparks sizzled down to the floor. The Prince, clicking his tongue, rubbed them into the carpet.

'Sometimes this place seems to be positively *crawling*,' he said. 'Do you have this problem where you live?'

'I can't say I do.'

'You're lucky,' the Prince said plaintively, rummaging in a cabinet. Jack had the sudden disconcerting impression that the Prince had become very old, wrapped in a collection of rags and feathers. 'Ah. Here we are.' He handed Jack a small, hard object wrapped in silk.

'What is it?' Jack asked.

'It's a penny,' the Prince said. 'It's the first penny ever made. Been in the family for years. I always knew there'd be a use for it one day.'

Carefully, Jack unwrapped the silk square. A tiny, ancient coin lay in the palm of his hand: uneven, the markings almost worn away. The remnant of a high-nosed profile ridged its pale surface.

'And this will free Madame Devi from the machine?'

'Oh, I think so. And you can take it, too. If you can.'

'I'm sorry?' Jack said, and at that moment the silk handkerchief flared into smoke. The penny was red hot, searing the skin of his palm, and he tossed it up, clutching at it desperately again and again. The Prince turned and laughed, soundlessly, and the dragons hissed and whispered

'Run...run...'

Grasping the hot penny, Jack bolted through the door of the music room. Hands reached out of the air, plucking at his coat and leaving trails of frosty snail-tracks across his skin. The penny was bitingly cold, numbing his palm, and he stumbled against the furniture. He ran through the parlour, through the dining room and when he reached the hallway he saw that one of the sidhe was waiting for him, rising halfway out of the carpet. Her hair streamed in a wind that he could not feel and as he came closer she opened her mouth to reveal a set of needle teeth. She snapped, clawing at him, and her nails scored his calf as he leaped. Her hair coiled around his ankles and nearly brought him down, but he was still running, sprinting for the door and the green light. Then the air was damp against his face and the gateway glowed ahead. The branches were full of faces, gazing at him, smiling thin, sharp smiles. Jack ran for the gateway, remembering at the last moment to turn backwards and stumble through. As he did so, he saw the Pavilion begin to turn in upon itself, its pale walls shimmering into nothingness until only a tiny, golden casket remained. And then he was through, falling out into the real rainy street with passers by staring at him and an old worn coin clutched tightly in his hurting hand.

The habit of flight was, it seemed, hard to break. Jack ran all the way down to the amusement arcade, flinging himself across the road and down the steps. He did not stop until he reached the arcade, where he stood panting, pain stitching through his side. The arcade was locked. Jack cursed under his breath. Inside his pocket, the penny was innocently cool. He juggled it indecisively in his palm. The double doors of the arcade were bolted but the window might be large enough to squeeze through...He'd never broken into anywhere before. Jack looked up and down the arcade. It was a horrible night, and no-one was about. He doubted whether the premises had a guard dog. Transferring the penny to the inner pocket of his jacket, he bundled his overcoat around his hand and punched through the glass. Guiltily, he broke off the remaining fragments and stuck his head through the opened space. The arcade was quite quiet. With difficulty, Jack squeezed through the gap and fell headfirst onto the grimy floor of the arcade.

The tarot machine was covered by a cloth, as though Madame Devi were a parrot. This seemed undignified, somehow. Jack frowned. Twitching the cloth aside, he peered in through the darkened glass. Madame Devi sat staring straight ahead, but he thought he detected a flicker in her shadowed eyes. Taking a deep breath, and willing it to work, Jack inserted the penny into the slot. For an instant, nothing happened, and then the glass walls of the booth shattered. They were not glass at all, Jack realised as he shielded his head, but ice. They hissed into steam as they fell and as he squinted beneath his raised arm he saw that Madam Devi, too, was melting. Her black waxen hair was flowing around her shoulders, shimmering into life, and her wan skin was flushed rosy with blood. She gave an immense, jaw-cracking yawn, revealing surprisingly sharp teeth, and smiled radiantly at her liberator. Then she fell off the stool. Jack managed to catch her before she hit the floor. She seemed to weigh nothing at all; he lifted her easily into his arms. Her golden eyes fluttered open, then closed as her languid head fell back against his sleeve.

Somehow, Jack's thoughts had not progressed beyond the actual liberation of Madame Devi from her confinement. Now, he realised, he had made himself responsible for her. She was light in his arms; indeed, she was almost weightless. Experimentally, he gave her a little upward push and she seemed to float for a moment, hovering above his outstretched hands before settling back like a butterfly. Jack carried her across to the bench and laid her down. As he did so, he noticed the end of a striped tail, twitching beneath the dusty silks. An old theatre programme lay on the bench; Jack fanned her rather ineffectually, but soon the golden eyes snapped open. Madame Devi smiled a pointed, captivating smile.

'It's been so long,' she whispered. 'So long…My home...my sisters...all gone.' A single ruby tear trickled down one cheek.

'Don't worry,' Jack heard himself say, with a sense of rising astonishment. 'You can stay with me. For as long as you like.'

'Why,' Madame Devi murmured. She made a little moue of modesty. 'Whatever made you think I was that kind of a girl?'

'I - I'm sorry - I didn't think -'

'But it's really terribly, terribly kind of you and I'd be <u>delighted</u> to accept...I just know you're a gentleman.'

'Ah, well, yes -'

Devi's eyes were yellow as fire; the air between them seemed to burn.

'Let's go now, shall we? It's so cold here...'

'Is - is there anything you'd like to take with you?' Jack said.

'No.' She held up her small velvet purse, and the Tarot pack. 'This is all I need.'

When Jack awoke next day, the storm had cleared and a shaft of pale winter sunlight gleamed through the window. The flat seemed warmer than usual, and as Jack swung his legs from under the blanket on the sofa, he experienced the novelty of not shivering. The bedroom door remained closed, but he could hear a muted humming emanating from within. He pottered into the kitchen and put the kettle on. The events of the previous day seemed like a dream. He made two cups of tea and took one of them to the bedroom door, where he gave a cautious knock. There was a moment's silence and then the door was flung open. Madame Devi stood in the entrance, wearing a negligee that was so encrusted with feathers it was hard to tell where silk stopped and maribou began. Her hair was piled in a complex Grecian knot at the back of her head; her eyes glittered in the sunlight.

'Darling!' Madame Devi breathed. 'Tea! How *exquisite*.'

'Sorry it's in a mug,' Jack muttered.

'Wonderful, wonderful...So long...' She took the tea from him and came to sit on the sofa. Glamour hung around her in an almost palpable miasma, but Devi seemed to be growing a little more subdued, somehow, like a child playing at dressing up.

'Is everything all right?' Jack asked, in concern.

'Jack...There's something I've been meaning to ask you. When you rescued me...how did you do it?'

Jack perched on the edge of the sofa and reached for her hand. Her fingers felt very frail in his own.

'Well,' he said, wondering quite where to begin. 'It was like this...'

He told her the story of the Pavilion, and the Prince, and the penny, and when he had finished he saw with a pang that Devi's dark face had grown grey.

'You see, I didn't ask you last night,' she whispered 'Because I was afraid of what you might say.'

'Devi, what's wrong?'

'A long time ago, Jack - a very long time ago - I was engaged to be married. It was arranged by my father, in the custom of my people. It wasn't something I wanted. So I ran away. Life with us isn't so different from yours, you know. My - fiancé - was angry, and he sent people to find me, and when he did he took me from my own world and imprisoned me in this one, in the form that you found me.'

'This fiance,' Jack said, with a rising sense of dismay. 'He wouldn't be the Prince of the Pavilion, now would he?'

There was a long pause, and then Devi whispered:

'Yes. If he hadn't wanted me to be free, Jack, he would never have helped you, we can be sure of that. And I don't think he's forgiven me, somehow. I was very - forceful - in the way that I expressed my reluctance to marry him.'

'We must get you away,' Jack said, firmly. 'Somewhere he can't find you, a place in which you'll be safe -'

'You don't understand. There isn't anywhere.' Her thin, hot fingers tightened around his own. Beneath the chair, the tip of a striped tail twitched unhappily. 'We'll just have to hope.'

They both jumped as the phone rang. It was Dolly.

'Jack? Mr Goldstein's just called. He's on his way back. There's a letter here - I think it's from the bank. Are you coming in today?'

'Er. I think so.'

'Well, look, I think you'd better see this before he gets here. It's important.'

'What time is it?' Jack asked.

There was a brief, frosty silence.

'It's *half past ten*, Mr O'Hanlon.'

'God!'

'I'm coming over,' Dolly said.

'No! Wait a minute - '

'I'll get a taxi.' - and then the phone was put down. To Devi, Jack said 'Don't worry. I'll get rid of her.'

'But no, darling. She said it was important; a letter from the bank…' Devi must have sharp ears, Jack thought. Her voice was filled with reproach. 'I only want to help, you know. After all, you helped me.' So Jack told her about the studio. It took some time; the concept of the cinema was an unfamiliar one to someone who'd been imprisoned in the nineteenth century. Belatedly, Jack realised that he was still clad in his dressing gown. He searched for his clothes and retreated into the bathroom, where he hastily changed. By the time he emerged again, Dolly was knocking at the door.

'Sorry to disturb you, Mr O'Hanlon,' Dolly said, in a voice that suggested she was anything but. 'I thought you ought to see this.' She held out the opened letter. Jack read it with a growing sense of dismay. Foreclosure on the studio. Perhaps Velma Merlin wouldn't have helped after all.

'Can I come in, Mr O'Hanlon?'

'Um.' Jack said, somewhat at a loss. Dolly, in her neat grey suit and spectacles, seemed to belong to a different world than his feather-clad guest. It was, however, too late. Clearly suspecting that matters were afoot, Dolly stepped smartly past him and into the living room. There was a short, charged silence.

'This is - well, this is Devi.'

'Charmed,' said the latter, extending a lavishly manicured hand. Dolly ignored it. She stared long and hard at Devi, even turning her head on one side to examine her from another angle. Turning to Jack, she said through tight lips

'Mr O'Hanlon, I hope you'll excuse me for saying this, but you're a fool.'

'It's not what you think!'

'Just fancy, we've been wasting our time on the likes of Velma Merlin when you've been hiding someone with real star quality!' Dolly snorted. 'Velma Merlin, indeed - she was born plain Ethel Simpson, I happen to know. And it showed. Not like the class act here.'

She turned to the dumbstruck figure of Madame Devi. 'When can you start? Do you have an agent?'

'Mr O'Hanlon,' Devi faltered, her hand fluttering at her throat. 'I seem to have a career.'

'Now we've just got time to get you down to the bank before poor Mr Goldstein gets here. I'm sure,' and here Dolly gave Madame Devi an even longer, harder look, 'that when the bank manager sets eyes on you, we'll have no more trouble from him.'

'Wait -' Jack said, stepping forward. His mind was whirling. On the one hand, it was marvellous that a glamorous leading lady had appeared at the moment the studio most needed one, but he hadn't gone to all that trouble to rescue Devi only to have her exposed once more to the Prince's ire. Besides, as glamorous as Devi was, there was no evidence that she could act. 'We need to think about this,' he said, but he saw with dismay that Devi was growing more brightly beneath Dolly's admiring gaze, as though soaking up the attention. Muttering placatory promises, he steered Dolly through the door and closed it behind her. 'If we're going to help you, Devi, we'll need to hide you from the Prince. Putting you on screen isn't exactly going to achieve that, is it?'

Devi sighed.

'I suppose not. But Jack, you have to know how it is for my kind. We live only for the attention of others. If no-one's looking at us, we dwindle, we fade. All those years trapped in the amusement arcade…you've no idea how terrible that was. It was only the Prince's spell that kept me alive. And I knew that if I married the Prince, he'd grow bored after a little while. He'd stop seeing me. All men do, after a time. I need an audience, Jack. I need to be seen.'

'I'll look at you,' Jack said, but she just gave a sad little smile. 'Anyway, there must be another way. The theatre, in America, maybe…'

'He'd still find me. No, Jack, this way is the safest. This way, with this new magical device - I can be seen, but no-one can touch me. It's perfect.' She rose from the couch and headed towards the hall, where Dolly was impatiently hovering.

The day seemed to Jack to pass in a whirlwind of activity. The visit to the bank, and the following loan arrangements, took an hour. The introduction of Dolphin Studio's latest star to the studio boss took all of five minutes. By mid-afternoon, Goldstein was back on the train to London, Devi in tow, to locate a suitable script. Left alone, Jack sat like a wrung rag in the lounge of the Grand Hotel, gasping into the perfumed air. Normally a person of some considerable energy, Jack was unused to feeling drained. He wondered whether he was simply being selfish, not wanting to share Devi with all these other people. Despite his loyalty to Goldstein, the studio was already taking second place in his affections. But he could not help feeling that what Devi was doing was dangerous.

'However did you find her?' Dolly was saying. Emotionally fraught as he was, Jack made no attempt at prevarication but simply told her. 'I don't quite know why I agreed to all this,' he finished, limply.

'Apsaras are always like that.'

'Pardon me?'

'Apsaras. That's what she is. I knew it as soon as I saw her. My old dad was out in India and he met one of them then. They're dancing girls -' Here Dolly, despite a career in the film industry, blushed slightly. ' - basically, but they're not human.'

Stupidly, Jack said 'They're not? No, I suppose they're not.'

'No, not at all. They're like demons, or the sidhe. They live for pleasure, and they've got Glamour. All their kind do. It's sort of protective coloration.' Dolly paused. 'It'll be a great asset in the movies, but you could end up doing whatever she wants you to do. She might seem sweet as pie now, but you want to keep an eye on her just the same.'

'Thanks,' Jack said, consideringly. 'I think I've already discovered that.'

A month later, production of *A Khyber Passion* was already underway. Madame Devi continued to sleep in Jack's bedroom; Jack continued to sleep on the sofa. She had filled the bedroom with a vast and motley array of costumes: silks and velvets and satins, weighed down with embroidery and beads. Feather boas hung from the curtain rail like a flock of limp birds; drifts of tulle and net covered the chairs like snow. All of this, it appeared, had come out of Madame Devi's little black purse.

'So pleased I kept it,' she murmured, surveying the display in the bedroom. 'Otherwise I wouldn't have a rag to my name...'

'You look beautiful,' Jack said. Despite Dolly's warnings, it was already much too late. He was utterly besotted. 'But listen, Devi - we still have to think about the Prince, you know. We have to work out a way to protect you.' Devi gave him a smile in reply and his mind seemed suddenly filled with cotton wool. He wondered, dimly, whether the story about the Prince and her marriage had even been true, but he couldn't seem to get a grip on his thoughts…' What are you doing to me?' he tried to say, but the room was filled with the fire of her eyes, and he could not think of anything any more.

Next day, his head seemed a little clearer. Excusing himself from the studio, Jack spent the morning in the public library, looking up all the mythologies he could lay his hands on. From a small red book published when the Raj was at its peak, he found a good deal of material about apsaras, and royalty. The book had been written too soon to take modern developments of technology into account, but certain of the comments made about the depiction of apsaras in Indian miniatures made Jack think. *Many have endeavoured to capture the likeness of an apsara, yet glamour is by its very essence impermanent...* Jack stared at the passage for some time. Then he checked the little book out of the library and took it back to the studio to study it. He did not, however, take it home.

Three days later, Jack sat in on the rushes for *A Khyber Passion*. Devi really was extraordinary, he thought, and so was the quality of the film that the cameraman was using. Rather than the usual grainy texture, the production seemed to flow smoothly from frame to frame, and the colours almost glowed. Devi's presence illuminated the screen. Beside Jack, Goldstein removed his cigar from his mouth in a moment of emotion and breathed

'Dynamite...This is going to make our *fortunes*...'

Jack could only agree, but there was unease behind his pride in Devi and he knew exactly where the source of it lay.

Finally, the movie was completed. They wrapped in late April, five months after Jack's fateful encounter in the amusement arcade. Jack attended the wrap party with his leading lady, half expecting trouble, but none came. After that, preliminary work began on Dolphin Studio's second feature. Although *A Khyber Passion* would not be released until the middle of June, Goldstein was confident that it would reap plaudits and rewards.

At the beginning of the second week in June, Jack arrived home to find a visitor. Devi was at some party in Town, and he had been working late at the studio. Unlocking the door, he stepped inside to be greeted by a most unseasonal chill. A drift of cobweb drapery brushed against his face. Unwillingly, Jack looked up. The pale, cold sidhe woman from the Pavilion was hovering upon his ceiling. Jack swallowed a lump of fear and said

'Why do you do that? And what are you doing in my hall, anyway?'

The sidhe's face cracked with a thin smile.

'But it's always so much warmer up here...And my kind can be so cold, don't you think? Or haven't you discovered that yet?'

'Just tell me what you want.'

'Why,' the sidhe whispered, sliding down the hall until her upside-down face was level with Jack's own. 'Why, I am sent with a warning. You see, my Prince has a long memory, and he does not understand pity or mercy, like all of my kind. You have caused this thing to be made. This pattern of images. And the most potent image of all is that of Her.' Jack did not need to ask who this might be. 'My Prince sends you a message. He says: if the images are displayed, then he will come and see them. He has a fancy to set foot again in the mortal world, among warm blood and hot flesh.' The sidhe's face betrayed a momentary, anguished longing. 'But if what he sees does not please him, then he will send the apsara's soul into her image forever and she will no longer walk the world. Our souls are more closely attached to us than your own, you see,' the sidhe said, and her features seemed to slip.

'So if the Prince doesn't like the film, he'll trap Devi inside it, the way he trapped her in the Tarot booth?' Jack said angrily. The sidhe smiled her icicle smile.

'And he is unlikely to be pleased.'

She began to melt, her face melting like wax too close to the flame.

'But if the film *does* please him,' Jack said, swiftly. He remembered the remarks about royalty in the little red library book. 'Or if something happens to change his mind, then I want him to promise that he'll leave Devi alone. I ask it in the name of his Father. And I charge you in the name of the Lords of the World to give him that message.'

The sidhe paused and her face looked suddenly as though it were melting.

'I will do so,' she said thickly, as though the words had been wrung out of her. And then she began to disappear.

'Wait!' Jack said, desperately, but she was already dissolving into the air and then was gone. Cursing, Jack stormed into the living room and phoned Goldstein.

'Great,' the producer said, when he heard Jack's story. 'So we have two options, don't we? Show the goddamn movie and we sell Devi out to her boyfriend's whim, or don't show it and lose all the backing. This could ruin us, Jack, like Velma Merlin never could. Shit. Well, it's not your fault. You did your best.'

'We'll have to see what happens,' Jack said stoically. Then he thought of the library book, and smiled, but it was a sad smile, nonetheless. The studio or Devi. If he was right, one of them would be lost, whatever events befell them over the next few days.

At some point during the night, Jack woke. Moonlight was pouring in through the window, sending blue shadows across the floor. Devi lay curled in the armchair, watching him, and in the moonlight, her eyes gleamed. *And my kind can be so cold, don't you think? Or haven't you discovered that yet?*

A Khyber Passion was screened in the Continental; that masterpiece of deco architecture which dominated the central section of the Brighton seafront. Stars of stage and screen trooped in to greet Goldstein and his crew and Devi, resplendent in a crimson gown which quite hid her tiger's tail, at once became the centre of attraction.

Shortly before the screening, however, a small group of people made their entrance. The rest of the audience, milling about the auditorium, stepped backwards like a parting sea to let them pass. The new arrivals were dressed in silks and velvets; feathers and lace, yet glimpsed from the corner of the eye, their finery seemed curiously dishevelled and tawdry. The person who walked in their midst was, however, immaculate.

'Oh my God,' Jack said, taking a swift step backwards, but it was already too late. The Prince turned.

'Mr O'Hanlon,' he said softly. There was the sudden glitter of a smile. 'How nice to see you.' Although Jack did not see him move, the Prince was suddenly at his side. He took Jack's arm in his own and began to lead him in the direction of the auditorium. 'I'm so looking forward to our night out,' he confided. 'We've really become such stay-at-homes...'

Jack looked over his shoulder to see a throng of faces: they all smiled at once, as though someone had pulled a string. Sharp teeth caught neon light.

There was an expectant hush as the lights of the cinema gradually dimmed. The Prince whispered into Jack's ear:

'Such a treat. A trip to the world of blood, and a chance for vengeance, all at the same time.'

'You said you'd only trap her soul if you didn't like the film!' Jack protested. The Prince sighed, as though troubled by some trifling reminder.

'I lied.'

Angrily, Jack turned and grasped the Prince's sleeve. The Prince stared at his hand as though he couldn't believe that Jack had dared to touch him.

'I sent your messenger back with a message of my own,' Jack snapped, before he had time to repent his own temerity. 'I charged you with a promise.' He was amazed to see that this time the Prince's gaze slid away from his own.

'And it will be kept,' the Prince murmured, icily. 'But only if this show should please me.'

'Or if something should happen to change your mind,' Jack reminded him, and after a moment, the Prince gave a small, curt nod. Behind them, the projector began to whirr. Jack watched miserably as the title and credits flickered onto the screen and then the first opening shot panned in across the echoing crags of the Khyber Pass. All archive footage, of course, or the Downs, but the audience weren't to know that. The battle scenes (the North West Frontier by way of Ditchling Beacon) began and within minutes the audience were on the edge of their seats. Even the Prince made an occasional start as the film ran on. Valentine Montgomery, generally known for supporting roles, made a splendid action hero. Wounded at last, he was carried to the palace where he would be cared for by Devi's character, and Jack found that he could not bear to watch. When would the Prince act: now or during the last reel, the climax of the film and Devi's life? Involuntarily, he closed his eyes. The audience gasped. Jack's breath caught in his throat. He thought of the crucial passage in the red book. *Many have endeavoured to capture the likeness of an apsara, yet glamour is an impermanent thing...*He forced his eyes open. The scene was a familiar one: Valentine Montgomery pale and suffering beneath the canopy, the lavish splendour of the palace behind him, but of Devi, there was no sign at all. It was a film without its heroine. Montgomery continued to give responses to a woman who was not there. Jack breathed a sigh like a collapsed balloon. Goldstein had sunk his head into his hands. The audience began to murmur amongst itself; at his side, Jack became aware of an arctic black gaze.

'Well?' the Prince hissed. 'Where is she?' Jack just shrugged.

'Glamour, you see. It doesn't last for long.'

Forcing himself to meet the Prince's eyes, he stared until the Prince himself began to contract inwards, diminishing into a small hot coal that sizzled on the velvet seat of the chair and then was gone. Silently, icily, his entourage drifted into motes of dust and sailed upwards into the light of the projector. Jack and the remainder of the audience were left to watch reel after baffling reel as the film unfolded for the next hour.

'What do you mean, it's a technical problem?' Goldstein asked, back at the studio. The cameraman spread his hands.

'It's Miss Devi's - enhancements, squire. What they call her Glamour. Must have worn off when the film was in the can.'

'But she's not totally illusory! Why doesn't she appear on screen as she is -um, without the Glamour?'

'Dunno, squire. She just hasn't.'

Unable to face Goldstein's woe at this further blow to the studio, Jack slipped off home. Devi was nowhere to be seen, and though he meant to wait up for her, he fell asleep on the sofa.

Next morning, Jack awoke to a thunderous knocking at his front door. Blearily, he opened it to find Goldstein standing on the step holding an armful of newspapers.

'Oh Christ,' Jack said hollowly. 'The reviews.'

Goldstein thrust a folded copy of the *Daily Globe* beneath his nose. Jack finally focused on the review headline: 'Surrealist masterpiece! Renaissance in avant garde cinema!'

'We have a hit!' Goldstein roared. 'Where's my leading lady? Or not, as the case may be. Listen, Jack. It's a whole new change of direction. We can make the films you've always wanted to. Art films. The critical establishment loves us. How about that?'

'We still won't make any money, though,' Jack said. 'Art films never do.' But he couldn't stop grinning, anyway, and neither could Goldstein.

When Goldstein finally left, Jack went back inside the flat to find Devi sitting on the sofa, gradually emerging from the air.

'I'm sorry,' she said. 'I let you down. I didn't mean to. I didn't <u>know</u>. My kind hasn't had much experience of your sort of magic.'

'It doesn't matter,' Jack said. 'I knew it might not work.' He told her about the library book and then about the Prince. 'At least you're still here.'

'Jack,' the apsara said in a whisper. 'Would you still - like me - even if I didn't look like this?'

'Of course I would. And I won't grow tired of you. I won't stop <u>looking</u>.'

'Well, then,' Devi said shyly, and slowly the glamour that she wore with the same assurance as she might don a feather boa or sealskin wrap began to fade and fall, until there was a small, dark woman sitting in the chair: unremarkable except for yellow eyes and a skinny, twitching tail.

'Listen,' Jack told her, because to his eyes it was true. 'I think you look great.' And then he kissed her.

This story was sponsored by Charles North

Hove Druid: I Stole Stone to Save Seagulls

Amazing claim of man in mascot's suit

by Evening Mercury reporter Nick Szczepanik

In an exclusive interview, Carl Tithe-Brokestoat, a 24-year-old unemployed Hove man, claimed to be the criminal mastermind behind the disappearance from Hove Park of the Goldstone, the mysterious rock that gave its name to the former home ground of Brighton and Hove Albion. At the same time, he claimed credit for the club's astonishing run to the second FA Cup Final in its history, becoming the first third division club to reach such a stage of the world's oldest competition.

Brokestoat, a self-proclaimed druid and self-confessed supporter of the club, alleges that the theft and subsequent destruction of the Goldstone was part of a mystical plan to return The Seagulls, as the club are known, to the pinnacle of British football that they last approached in 1983, the previous occasion on which they reached the FA Cup final.

According to Brokestoat, the Goldstone, which disappeared last December, was removed by himself and a small band of associates, one of whom had access to a JCB and other heavy equipment. The stone, weighing some twenty tons and believed by Brokestoat and his acolytes to have magical properties, was then partially ground down into powder and some of it spread on the pitch at Withdean Stadium, the current temporary home of the Albion. The mystical qualities claimed by Brokestoat for the stone are, he says, behind the transformation in the team's fortunes since the January thaw. The remainder of the stone is now at a secret location. 'There is plenty more stone where that came from,' he told our reporter.

Incredible as it may seem, certain strands in Brokestoat's astonishing story can be confirmed. Our investigations confirm that he has indeed been the leader of a breakaway druidical sect in Hove for some years, although some of his beliefs are at variance with what may be termed mainstream druidism. 'We dissociate ourselves completely from this man,' said a spokesman for the Order of Bards, Ovates and Druids, whose National Representative Office is to be found, by coincidence, in Portslade. 'We especially deplore the sacrilegious vandalism he has perpetrated on a holy relic, namely the Goldstone.'

Another part of Brokestoat's apparently fantastic allegations can also be confirmed. It is true, as he claims, that he had a brief spell as the Albion mascot, 'Gully', an eight-foot tall seagull. Brokestoat was also revealed as the chief instigator behind a flood of letters calling for the return of the mascot, previously seen at The Goldstone Ground in the early 1990s.

Brokestoat hatched his plot about a year ago. Unlike 99 percent of the club's followers, he believed that there was more to its indifferent displays on the pitch than poor management and its lack of a permanent home since the demolition of the old Goldstone Ground following its sale and conversion into retail outlets, all destroyed in the mysterious fires of last year.

'It was obvious to me as a druid that the club was missing the close connection with the Goldstone itself, a source of mystic power that had originally lain under the pitch, but which was moved into Hove Park across the road in 1906,' Brokestoat said. 'That, however, was close enough for its power to work, and it is significant that the North Stand, the area of the ground where the most loyal and vocal supporters used to stand, was the side nearest Hove Park and the Stone. It had given the team the power to rise to the old first division in the 1970s and reach the 1983 Cup Final. Unfortunately, Hove Council's conversion of some nearby tennis courts into an Astroturf pitch a few years later confused it; it didn't know which footballers to help, and its power was dissipated.' As Brokestoat says, following the conversion of the tennis courts, the team's fortunes slumped and the club avoided relegation to the Conference by the skin of its teeth.

Things hardly improved after the sale of the ground, when the team was forced to play matches at Gillingham, too far away for the Goldstone to exert any influence at all. 'People said that it was going to be like playing 46 away games instead of 23, which had the alarm bells ringing with me, because Albion have always had such a terrible away record compared to most other teams,' said Brokestoat. 'So much of their strength, you see, has come from the Stone.'

However, Brokestoat had what he describes as a brainwave, and it was about this time that our letters column began to be deluged with requests for the return of the Gully mascot, reluctantly acceded to by the club. The return was not a success, as Gully spent more time pacing the pitch at Gillingham's Priestfield Stadium than entertaining young supporters, its ostensible purpose. Brokestoat can now explain.

'That was me in the Gully suit, and my followers and myself that wrote all the letters. When the Goldstone Ground was being demolished, I broke in one night and found the old Gully costume buried behind the apprentices' toilets and put it in the back of my van just in case. It was made of foam rubber and feathers, with a fibre-glass beak. It was a bit tatty and dusty, and it smelled a bit - I think something had been nesting in it at some stage - but I sponged it down and it was almost as good as new, from a distance anyway. Then I hatched the first of my plans.'

As the man in possession of the Gully costume, Brokestoat was in a unique position to apply for the mascot's job. In fact, to his surprise and relief, he was the only contender for the position. It now seems that while apparently wandering aimlessly around the Priestfield Stadium playing surface instead of supervising the Southwick Round Table under-12 penalty shoot-out, Gully/Brokestoat was, in fact, casting runic spells on the pitch, but to little effect. The team's fortunes improved only a little.

His next prank, and the one for which he was banned from The Priestfield Stadium for life, was, frankly, distasteful.

'After consulting the runes, I realised where I had been going wrong,' Brokestoat recalls. 'Spells by themselves were all well and good, and probably earned us a point or two, but no more. For example, I believe they were responsible for that Hartlepool defender lowering his shorts to the linesman and getting sent off after a dodgy throw-in award. At half time in that game I had tried out a new ire-inducing incantation at the end we were due to attack, although I had really hoped it would make our forwards more aggressive. In general, though, the effects were not as strong as I intended. I realised that I had to bring the players into direct contact with the Goldstone itself, the source of the team's power for most of their history.

'I originally took scrapings from the stone and ground them down hoping to put them into the players' tea at half-time, but I wasn't allowed into the dressing room; something about the goalkeeper being allergic to feathers. So I did the next best thing, and put it in my own tea. Then, when no-one was looking, I transferred it to the pitch in the most direct way possible.'

His initial success, on that rainy evening when Albion beat Brentford, the league leaders, 7-1, led him to attempt to repeat the trick the following Saturday, when the team entertained Swansea City - unfortunately, a dry, sunny afternoon.

'In the driving rain the night of the Brentford match, nobody noticed a bit of extra pitch-watering, but there were complaints when I did what I knew I had to on the Saturday,' Brokestoat said. 'Funnily enough, nobody objected when Barry Fry did the same in all four corners of the pitch at Birmingham City when he was manager there, to lift a gypsy curse.' Fry, of course, did not choose a match day when thousands of supporters were in the ground.

Regular readers of these pages will no doubt remember that Brokestoat only evaded prosecution for a public order offence when he was able to produce medical evidence of an incontinence problem. He can now reveal that the doctor who provided the evidence has druidic sympathies. However, the incident and a fight between Gully and Swansea's mascot, Cyril the Swan, which went unreported but, Brokestoat revealed exclusively to us, took place in the players' tunnel at half time and resulted in one of the referee's assistants suffering a bruised elbow and a broken flag, meant the end of the club's experiment of bringing back Gully.

Brokestoat blames the altercation in the tunnel on his beliefs. He is an animist, as are many druids, and believes that there is a little of the animal, or bird in his case, in all of us. 'That pathetic swan mascot came up to me at half-time and said it was a good thing I'd only wet myself and did I have white shit like a real seagull. I don't know what came over me. It was as if I had been possessed by the spirit of a real seagull, and saw the swan as an enemy on my territory. We druids, of course, are very close to nature. There is a risk.' The upshot was that Brokestoat was left to ponder alternatives while the team's form remained poor.

Meanwhile, negotiations were afoot to speed the return of the team to Brighton, specifically Withdean Stadium, and Brokestoat took an active role in gathering support for the move. However, his work, he says, went further than gathering names for petitions. He was present in council meetings when key planning decisions were taken, and used his powers, he believes, to influence wavering councillors.

'Druidic power can influence weak minds, and some of the members of the council were wavering, and therefore especially susceptible to suggestions. Mind you, some of them were also just plain weak-minded, which helped.'

When the Albion began their stay at Withdean by holding Nottingham Forest to a draw in their opening friendly match then won their first league game there 6-0, Brokestoat believed that all was well again, and that no further intervention on his part would be necessary. Unfortunately, it soon became obvious that the encouraging early results were simply the effect of the excitement generated by the return to Brighton, an excitement that wore off rapidly.

Another member of Brokestoat's sect, however, provided an answer. As a worker with the Parks and Gardens department of Brighton and Hove Council, he had access to heavy equipment and, better still, to the Stadium itself. During the heavy snows of last winter that caused the closure of the Newtimber and Falmer passes and main London railway line for several days, effectively cutting Brighton and Hove off from the rest of the country, this equipment was idle, and Brokestoat persuaded the man to allow members of the sect to remove the Stone. The next morning, snowboarders and sledgers in the park were astonished to see a gaping hole where the Goldstone had been.

'We originally considered removing only odd chunks at a time, but when I first took scrapings it left an obvious scar, and my mole in Parks and Gardens had overheard council officers talking about vandalism,' Brokestoat explained. 'We could not take the risk that the Stone would be placed behind protective fencing or Perspex screens, so we realised it was all or nothing. We had to take the entire Stone to a place of safety.

'Like an iceberg, much of it was underground and it was a far more difficult job than we had anticipated. However, our predecessors built Stonehenge without the assistance of heavy earth-moving plant, so we were unlikely to be stymied by the prospect of moving something so tiny, relatively speaking.' Brokestoat would not reveal the present whereabouts of the Stone, although he said that it was not on Parks and Gardens property. He confirmed that council equipment, however, was used to spread the ground, powdered Stone on the Withdean pitch once the thaw had set in. 'The same machines they use for spreading grass seed and fertiliser,' he revealed.

Whether it was the new top dressing or not, the performance of the team after its enforced winter break was, as everyone knows, mesmeric. A glut of postponements caused by the snows meant that the club's delayed FA Cup second round tie at home to Plymouth Argyle was the first match on the newly-impregnated surface, and Albion romped home 4-1. That brought Reading to Withdean in the third round the following week, and they were dispatched 3-0. Because FA Cup ties take precedence over league fixtures, Albion, instead of journeying to Carlisle, found themselves entertaining Leicester City eight days later, in front of the cameras of Sky TV. The football world looked on amazed as Darren Freeman, the Brighton-born forward, scored the only goal of the match before the players settled down to listen to the draw for the fifth round. 'Anyone at home,' was the wish of manager Micky Adams.

And of course, it was a home tie, against Charlton Athletic, who were in the middle of a run of 12 successive league victories. They, however, had no answer to the Albion's irresistible cup form nor, according to Brokestoat, of the ground-up Goldstone. 'We were able to top it up before every home match, just to keep the power at optimum level,' Brokestoat explained. The sixth round victory over Chelsea, again at Withdean, has already passed into the club's legends. Foreign internationals such as Desailly, Leboeuf and Zola had no answer to the homespun skills of Cullip, Oatway and Mayo.

'It was partly that, and partly an extra incantation traditionally used to help repel invaders, which we chanted over the spreader just before treating the pitch,' Brokestoat said.

Brokestoat cannot claim any mystic intervention before the semi-final victory over Bolton Wanderers, which was staged at a neutral ground, although he offers an alternative explanation.

'Bolton were just crap,' he said. However, it begs the question of how Brokestoat can hope to influence the outcome of the final against Newcastle United, Alan Shearer and all, at Wembley, where security is watertight before a major game. Brokestoat winked knowingly when we raised the matter and we anticipated some hints at least of his plans to cover the lush Wembley pitch with essence of Hove Park, but he abruptly changed the subject to special offers for weekend hire of the Good Year blimp, so we were disappointed.

We have presented Brokestoat's story exactly as told to us, but in our opinion it is nothing more than that - a story. Brokestoat is well-meaning, and has gone to great lengths to make his hoax believable. Indeed, he probably believes it himself. To most of us, though, the idea of a mystic influence deciding the outcome of the most famous competition in the world is laughable compared to the simple truth that a team in the lower half of the third division can suddenly find the form necessary to beat two Premiership clubs and the first division leaders. That is less a question of the alleged magic of an obscure Celtic religion than the well-documented Magic of The Cup.

The only sour note of our interview came as we were about to leave. Brokestoat wondered if we would care for a snack before we left. 'A little raw fish, perhaps?' he enquired. Sushi, we said, was not quite what we associated with druids - Buddhists, perhaps. 'No, not sushi,' he said, 'but I've got a few sprats and a piece of cod. When I was the mascot we played at Grimsby and Hull and some local comedian thought it would be highly amusing to throw fish to a seagull. Some of it got caught in the costume and I was feeling a bit peckish during the second half, so I tried a bit. I've developed quite a taste for it. As I said, it's my druidic empathy with the spirit of the seagull...'

We made our excuses and left.

To Walk Upon the Sea

Larry Matthews

It was her eyes. Jez watched her gradually assume control, as if it were another piece of the diving equipment they were donning. There was something in Suzy's eyes, as well as the way she was directing proceedings. Underwater it was her world: she was always dive leader of their buddy pair and what she said - or signalled - went. It was the one area of their life together where she did take control.

They were rocking at anchor in a small inflatable on the open sea, with Brighton and the cliffs of the coast just visible to the north. To the west the pier was a thin black line on the horizon. Jez looked around. There were no other boats for miles in any direction.

He looked again at Suzy, busily checking the equipment and consulting dive tables. He had watched her surreptitiously as they rode the pier train mile after mile out to sea, but the tension of the previous night seemed to have gone. He was still mildly irritated at her stubbornness in not telling what she was going to show him, but it wouldn't be long now. Anyway, who could bear grudges on a day like this? The morning was bright and clear, with a gentle swell on a smooth sea: perfect weather.

They entered the water by tipping themselves backwards over the grey rubber tubes at the sides of the inflatable and all his worries were swept away, as they always were, by the thrilling embrace of the cold water seeping into his wetsuit, the thin layer tingling his skin until it warmed up to his body temperature. His training took over: the deep slow breathing, the checking of the gauges. They finned down the anchor rope and then off to the east. They were in a blue-grey world, cruising along a few metres above the sandy seabed, dim light percolating down from the surface far above. Visibility was ten metres or so, good for the Channel. The world opened up before them as they swam, and closed again behind them.

Suzy swam on, glancing from time to time at the instruments on her wrist, and Jez followed slightly behind and above. He drifted off into a reverie, working his legs alternately, up, down, up, down, smoothly to conserve energy and air. All the tension had gone out of him too; the tension that had been there since the argument of the previous night when he had wanted to tell her about his problems at Nuland. She had criticised Nuland once again, forcing him into the company's defence, which was uncomfortable since he was feeling ambivalent enough himself about his employer. It was easy enough for Suzy to toe the 'Friends of the Sea' line on everything, but things weren't that simple. If -

His mind came to with a snap, in mid stroke. Suzy had pulled up and was hanging there, looking at him, and pointing. He looked. A dolphin!

Suzy was smiling, he could see it in her eyes. Now there were two dolphins: bottlenose, Jez thought, about three metres long. The dolphins approached them, and he could hear the clicks and chirrups of their sonar as they wheeled and circled, twisting around, upside down, right way up, looking at him from all angles, and finally swam languidly off. Suzy signalled that they should follow. Jez noticed stones and rocks on the sandy bottom, which looked almost as if they had been laid out in deliberate patterns.

He watched dumbfounded as one of the dolphins swam up with a stone in its beak, dropped it onto the sand and nuzzled it into position. It then regarded him as if expecting him to respond in some way. He felt a touch on his arm: Suzy was urging him further on. He followed her, leaving the dolphins behind, then stopped when she did so. She pointed down. Laid out on the seabed, made up of stones and rocks placed on the sand, was a map of the local coastline.

Another, larger, dolphin emerged from the haze. It also circled them, looking and clicking from a variety of angles. It went up to Suzy, who seemed to exchange signals with it, and it then returned to Jez. He tried to keep it in sight as it circled him, but lost sight of it behind him. He felt a nudge on his tank. Alarmed, he twisted round. But the dolphin was already back looking into Suzy's mask. The dolphin repeated the performance, effortlessly manoeuvring round Jez's twisting body to tap on his tank. Jez was worried: if the dolphin suddenly took it into its head to pull on his air hose, or bite through it …

Then Suzy was looking into his face, concerned about something. She took hold of his wrist to look at his instruments, and signalled unease to him; the palm down fluttering of the hand. Then came the signal for sharing air from her tank. She took her mouthpiece out of her mouth, gestured to him and replaced it, taking two breaths, then offered it to him. Trust me, her eyes said. She was holding tightly onto him with her other hand. He began to get worried.

He looked at his instruments. Plenty of air left. What on earth was she doing? He shook his head: there was no point in taking any risks, no reason to share air from Suzy's tank. She was still agitated about something, though. He had better get her to the surface. He pointed upward with his thumb. She shook her head violently, offered him her mouthpiece again.

He continued to urge her upwards, but she struggled, broke free, and swam off a few paces, then returned, held onto him and offered him her mouthpiece again. He was distinctly worried now: this was definitely not like her. He decided to humour her, and took the mouthpiece, took two breaths, gave it back: the buddy air-sharing drill. His own mouthpiece he held at his side. At last she seemed to relax, and gave him the OK sign of finger and thumb, then a thumbs up. With some relief he kicked slowly and they began to rise. At least they were heading for the surface now. She rose with him, still holding on to him, as they passed the mouthpiece back and forth. He looked at his gauges: still thirty metres to go. But if they kept calm, it would be all right.

Accept the mouthpiece, breathe out in out in, then give it back, over and over again. He lost count, but they were into a rhythm now. He started to relax slightly, and only then realised how tense he had been. Accept, out in out in, give …accept, out in out in, give ….

He looked up: the surface was dappled sunlight above them. At five metres Suzy pointed to his wrist gauge and indicated a decompression stop. He signalled agreement and they hung in the water, still exchanging the mouthpiece, while they timed five minutes.

When they broke surface, they both gasped and inflated the buoyancy bags on their suits. 'OK?' Suzy shouted.

'OK. What was all that about?'

'Let's just get to the boat.' She pointed: it was some hundred metres away. He turned to her but she had already fitted her snorkel and was slowly finning towards the boat. There was nothing to do but follow her.

They struggled into the boat, shedding their tanks and fins, and collapsed to catch their breath. Jez usually felt particularly alive after a dive, but this time he felt exhausted. Suzy examined his face, took his hand to look at his fingernails, and apparently satisfied, flopped back against the side of the boat.

'What was all that about?' he asked again. She just glared at him.

'Suzy?'

'You saw my signals.'

'But …'

'If I signal to share air, we share air, OK?'

'But why? You know I had a full tank - '

'Never mind why. Who was dive leader?'

'Look, what was - '

'Who was dive leader?' she insisted, more loudly.

'You were.'

'Then you should have trusted me.'

'But I thought - '

'If I'm dive leader you have to trust me.' It was as if she were speaking to a child.

He sighed. 'I know. I'm sorry.'

'Good.' She seemed to relax. Droplets sprayed from her hair as she shook her head and ran a towel over it. 'The dolphin signalled to me that there was something wrong with your air.'

'What?'

'You heard me.'

'What do you mean, something wrong?'

'I don't know. But I've told you they can see inside solid objects with their sonar. Anyway I trust them. We can have a look at the tank when we get back.'

She started the motor headed the boat towards the pier. He remembered the map of stones. 'But how did the dolphin know … I didn't realise … what signals do you use, I mean ... I didn't dream it, did I?'

'It's real. We've got further with the research than we ever hoped.'

'How? When?'

'I'll tell you more later. Not now.'

'What? Why not? Don't you trust me?'

She just looked at him. Those big brown eyes. There was no way to unsay what he'd just said.

'Suzy …' But she just stared ahead, hand on the tiller. Questions burned in his mind. They sped on in silence, with just the drone of the outboard to accompany their thoughts. The tense silence persisted while they reached the pier, stowed their gear and waited for the train along the pier back to land. Once on the train Suzy seemed more at peace; she still signalled for silence, but now it was more as if frightened of being overheard.

He closed his eyes. He had wanted to tell her for days about Pete Goodman and the sea-freezing and everything, but every time he started they ended up in an argument, and frankly he was growing tired of the chiding over working for Nuland. Since last night, when she had declared that she had something to show *him*, there had been all this secrecy as well.

The train slowed and paused at Twomile station, and Jez looked around idly at the scene. The pier here opened out into a wide disc of housing, retail and catering space, all supported on a base of piles and girders: such conventional developments had been Nuland's main business in the early days, before it had developed its sea-solidifying technology. Solidification had enabled strips of coastal land to be created out of nothing: a fabulous business, the price of land being what it was. Yet the full potential had never been realised because of the vested interests of the owners of the coastal strip: if you had a sea-front property you would resist someone building on the sea in front of you. The developers were winning the battle - Jez had seen the same game played out with conventional land reclamation in Holland and Hong Kong - but it was a slow, laborious struggle. Or had been until now …

The train picked up speed for the final leg to Palace station at the landward end of the pier. This close to land the details of the coast became visible: first buildings, then vehicles and finally people on the seafront. At Palace station they collected together their gear, still without speaking. Outside, though, the fresh air seemed to revive Suzy's spirits. They wandered down onto the beach and sat on the pebbles near the shoreline.

It was a beautiful afternoon and the silver-grey rippling surface of the sea nearby blended in the distance into a calming dappled texture. The right hand half of the view was pierced by the pier striding off into the distance and over the horizon. The relentless extension of the pier reminded him of films he had seen of the railways pushing into the old American West. Meanwhile the allure of Midway station had attracted copious investment and Nuland was erecting its new headquarters building there. He supposed that at some point he would have to move out there from his office near Twomile station; he didn't relish the longer commute this would mean.

He waited and at last Suzy started to talk.

'You know that for some time we've been applying semiotic technology with the wild dolphin research group. With the film industry people and the new media people, Brighton's the place to be at the moment. And as dolphins are now coming back to the Channel in larger numbers … '

Jez nodded. 'Friends of the Sea have sponsored the research programme; yes, you've told me all this.'

'Sorry, I didn't mean to lecture. Well, a couple of weeks ago we started to make real progress with the dolphins. Incorporating pressure waves was the breakthrough. All of a sudden it was as if they took over. They've taught us *their* signals as much as the other way around. We're finding out about their culture - did you know they sometimes herd whales, like we ride elephants? We're just starting to scratch the surface …'

'But this is fantastic,' Jez said. 'It's your dream come true, isn't it? Why haven't you told - well, the government, the media?'

'The Fots highups won't allow it.'

'Why on Earth not?'

'They say they want to be sure this time, after all the false alarms. Everybody's been sworn to secrecy.' She sighed. 'It's been terrible not being able to tell you! I shouldn't have taken you out today, really. Only they're getting more and more concerned about Nuland, and I thought …'

'Aren't you afraid I'll tell everybody?'

'No. I know you better then that.'

'You said - '

'I know I did. I was angry.'

'Wait a minute. Concerned about Nuland, did you say?'

'Yes, Jez. They have a problem with the sea-freezing.'

'Who do?'

'The dolphins.'

'Hmph.' Jez looked out to sea. 'But, what's the problem? Is their habitat threatened so much, now all of a sudden? Surely the land-take is tiny.'

'No, it's not that. Somehow the phase shifting affects them.'

'You mean, phase shifting as in the solidification process?'

'Yes. They say they do something similar in some way themselves, I think, but we're not sure what. Anyway it causes them pain. Something out at Pierhead is particularly bad.'

'But I don't see … I mean phase shifting's just a realignment of hydrogen bonds triggered by a patterned electric field. The field drops off with distance like everything else. An inverse square law. I don't see how it should affect dolphins in the open sea.'

'Well don't look at me,' said Suzy wearily. Jez looked out to sea again. It looked normal enough to him.

The sun was sinking into the sea behind the pier, and it was beginning to get cold. There was a lot to take in, and he felt he needed to digest it all. He asked, as he often did, where she wanted to eat. She replied, as she always did, 'You choose.' On an impulse, Jez suggested Nuland Tower. Suzy grimaced but agreed, and so instead of walking up into the Lanes they took a tram along the seafront.

The area of new land next to the old marina was Nuland's pride and joy: a showcase for solidification. As they walked from the tram station across to the main tower, Jez still found it hard to believe that several metres down under the tarmac and topsoil he was walking on solid seawater. He still found the whole thing amazing, and often wandered in to see the demonstration tank in the PR centre near his office at Twomile station. He was well known to the staff there as he sat in with them in the control room overlooking the tank, watching the visiting dignitaries or groups of the public who would surround the large tank of sea water and gasp as the switch was thrown, the water solidified in an instant, and one of the group would be invited to test their weight on it.

At the main tower they took the lift to the observation deck, and ended up in the revolving restaurant there. From their table the view was stunning, spreading out in all directions from the floodlit marina a hundred metres beneath their feet. As their table was carried slowly around the tower, they gazed out in turn over the lights of Brighton, then its dark hinterland, then the coast to the east, and finally the sea. The sea itself was black, with just a scattering of ships' lights and the pier, a thin straight line of light extending to the horizon.

Suzy sighed and said, 'Just imagine if it was all frozen ...'

'Solidified,' Jez said, then scowled, annoyed at himself. Nuland had been trying to erase the word 'frozen' from public use ever since market research had identified the latent public fear that something frozen might one day melt. Jez went along with it, out of duty, although he felt it was a hopeless, Canute-like gesture; but he felt he shouldn't let the habit intrude into a conversation with Suzy.

'Sorry,' he said. 'Anyway, listen, I wanted to talk to you about that: I've found something out at Nuland.'

'Nuland again! I'm fed up with Nuland.'

'Look, I know you don't like big corporations ...'

'Especially ones that are eating into the sea.'

'Oh, come on, the areas are minuscule.'

'But it won't stop until the seas are all paved over.'

Something flared in him. 'Oh, nonsense! It's all right for you; I have to live in the real world.'

She looked away.

'Sorry, Suzy, I didn't mean that.'

She turned to him again. 'It's the *real* world that Nuland's destroying! The seas - that's the real world, not your silly corporate games.'

He sighed. 'I know. But look, it's difficult for me - ' She snorted.

'Yes, Suzy, it is! See it from my point of view for once.' Jez took a breath. She wasn't normally like this. 'Look, I sympathise with what you're doing at Friends of the Sea, even before all ... this. If sea-freezing is affecting dolphins then that's terrible. But Nuland's not all bad.'

'No?'

'No. They've saved millions of lives in Bangladesh. And the electric sandbags - even your Dad's got some for his house in Chichester.'

She bridled immediately. 'You see, you're taking their side again!'

'That's not fair. You eat here, you enjoy this view, it's all due to Nuland. We use my salary ...'

She leapt to her feet. 'Keep your precious salary!' she shouted, and stormed out.

Jez sat open-mouthed, then ran after her. 'Suzy, Suzy...' But she was gone.

He stood looking at the closed outer lift doors for a while, and then slowly returned to the table, and sat staring out of the window, unseeing. Like the table, his life seemed to be showing him interesting views, but to be going round in circles. He remembered how he had felt at the start of his career, fresh out of college, and how he was going to change the world. It had really felt like that in the early days. But it was all muddier now, and he had seen both sides to Nuland. He hadn't wanted to change the world by harming dolphins. When the waitress dropped the bill on the table in front of him, half an hour had passed. It was enough. He had decided that Suzy was ultimately right.

He would show her.

* * * * *

Like a galaxy alive, silver sparks danced against a black background. Jez brooded with his mind in neutral, then stirred himself and focused his eyes. It was early evening. The galaxy resolved itself into flashes of moonlight on the dark sea below as the train sped along the pier towards the coast. He looked up: they were coming up to Twomile Station and the lights of Brighton were strung along the horizon ahead. Two miles in which to get his thoughts straight.

In the two days since the dive he had come no closer to working out what he has going to do, in practical terms. The foundations of his relationship with Suzy had been looking somewhat shaky too. At first she had refused his calls, but then this morning she had called about his air tank. The lab she had sent it to had found something, but were refusing to say what. It had shaken Jez, even though the medical check-up which Suzy had insisted on had given him the all-clear.

The train reached Palace station and Jez emerged into the bustling concourse at the front of the pier. He looked for Suzy and found her sitting on a bench looking out to sea.

It was the old Suzy, at least. But after a quick cross examination on his health, she didn't want to talk over the situation right away.

'I just want to be with you, do something normal for an hour or two,' she said. So they went to The Saxon Drugs, their usual pub in the Lanes. The pub was as lively as usual, but it was not easy to keep up small talk with the air tank looming in the background. After a while they both felt the need for some fresh air, and walked down to the sea front again, out onto the beach. By this time it was dark but a crescent moon was up. The beach was deserted.

'So what was this about Nuland that you were going to tell me?' she asked.

'Well… I've a feeling that this will make matters worse. They've found a fixer - a sort of binding agent - to make solidification permanent. So that when the current is switched off the solidification phase change remains. They're going to try trial it at Nuland Tower when it's shut for grid maintenance next weekend.'

Up to now solidified water had gradually 'melted' - whatever Nuland said, there was no other word for it - when the current was switched off: for permanent structures the power grid had to be kept electrified, albeit it with a tiny voltage, with an array of power sources and backups. The blocks of seawater from the demo tank which were dumped into the sea all degraded over a period of a few days. Jez remembered on one of his dives with Suzy seeing them on the sea floor piled against the base of the pier structure, crumbling cubes of solid water, almost invisible against their liquid surroundings. They had reminded him of making jelly as a child, melting the small cubes in hot water.

'So?' asked Suzy.

'Well, if the fixing agent works it will make solidification a lot more acceptable and there'll be a rapid expansion of it. It'll really take off. Sooner or later they won't be tied to the coastal fringes either.'

'But it's hurting the dolphins! And who knows what other problems it would cause? Why can't they wait until we know more about it?'

'I know, but they don't think like that. The economic forces are overwhelming. Everything happens a bit at a time, and people are too greedy at each stage. Until suddenly it's too late.' Jez felt a familiar discomfort, explaining how the world worked and knowing that it sounded like he condoned it.

'They're paranoid about secrecy too,' Jez went on. 'There's a test rig at Pierhead; I stumbled onto it while I was out there last week and the next thing I knew I had Goodman having a quiet word with me about my career prospects and what was good for me.'

'Goodman?'

'Pete Goodman. Head of Security. Scary bloke.'

'Why would they worry about secrecy?'

'Well, the fixing agent seems to work at lab scale and at test sites. But Nuland Tower would be very public if anything went wrong. Also, in fact I guess more importantly, handling the timing of any announcement would be a huge issue for the share price.'

Suzy looked puzzled. 'Sorry, I can't get my mind round this at the moment. I'm worried about the dolphins. If the current can be switched off wouldn't that be good?'

'It depends on what's affecting them, the current or something else. Do you have any idea about what the problem is?'

'No. We think it might have something to do with the paralimbic lobes.'

'Say that again.'

'We think it's to do with the paralimbic lobes. They're a feature of cetacean brains. What's the matter?'

'I've heard that word before. One group were talking about it at Pierhead, and changed the subject rather obviously when I turned up. But I didn't think anything of it.'

Suzy's eyes widened. 'Do you think they *know* about the effect on dolphins?

'I don't know. Gee, if they do, it'd be seen as real bad news. They might even try to suppress it.'

'Surely they couldn't?'

'I wouldn't put it past them to try. If they can once get it going, the vested interests behind them would be staggering.'

Suzy shivered. 'I've just had an awful thought. Do you think the business with the air tank might not have been an accident?'

'You mean … no, that would be being paranoid.' But suddenly Jez wasn't so confident. There would be billions at stake.

Suzy sat up. 'We've got to do something,' she said.

'Yes,' said Jez. He waited until it sank in.

'Yes?'

'Yes. Don't look so surprised. I'm on your side really, you know.'

She hugged him. 'Oh, Jez…' Then, 'What do we do?' As if he would know. Which was gratifying, but wrong.

'I don't know,' he admitted. 'I mean, we could tell people. But our campaigners ...'

'We can do that too. But - I don't know. I feel as if I want to do something directly, use my inside knowledge if you like. You're always saying everyone should do their bit. It's as if I'm in the right place at the right time, somehow.'

'I don't know, Jez ... What would you do, anyway? Sabotage something?'

'Hmph.'

'Well, what then?'

'I don't *know*.' Jez thought. 'To make a real difference, you'd need to get the public on your side.'

'Surely if we told people - '

'You can't rely on people doing the right thing. I'm sorry, Suzy, but you can't: Fots has found that out. I think you have to get people scared. Say you convinced them that solidification was unsafe, or dangerous, like with the ice-nine scare in the early days, remember? Like the food scares. And you'd need something to scare them about. Even then you might only delay things for a while.'

'We.'

'What?'

'*We* would only delay things. But it would buy time. It sounds as if it might make all the difference.'

Jez had to smile. There seemed to be no reason in the world to be hopeful, but he felt wonderful anyway. He stared out to sea. The all too liquid sea - but for how long?

* * * * *

Jez leaned back in his chair; it was well after hours and it was quiet in his office. As far as he knew, Suzy and he were the only people in the building. He had spent forty minutes making the list of calls he had planned out, pulling strings, trading on his credibility with the operations people to persuade them to call the alert and evacuate not just Nuland Tower, but the whole solid-sea complex for the duration of the test. Now it was all in motion. There was a noise behind him. He turned.

'Suzy...'

But it was Goodman. He was standing at the doorway. Suzy stood there too, looking apologetic.

Goodman was a thick-set ex-military man who had found a lucrative outlet for his talents by moving to the private sector. It seemed totally incongruous for him to be here in person, dressed in a leather jacket and jeans: Jez associated him with three piece suits and the corridors of power.

'I'm disappointed,' said Goodman, coming into the office. Jez got up to face him. Goodman approached and tried to see past Jez to the desk. 'Just what are you two up to, anyway?' he asked. 'I notice you've been making rather a lot of calls.'

Jez started to edge back in front of the desk, but Goodman just smiled. 'Calls get logged, you know,' he said. He reminded Jez of a snake.

Jez remained silent. He could hear the sea lapping against the pier structure below.

'It's a pity,' Goodman continued, 'that people don't stick to their own business. The world is full enough of troubles as it is. Diving accidents for example. They happen all the time, I'm told.'

'You ...'

Goodman just looked at him. He had stopped smiling. 'You're out of your league,' he said. 'Now, what is it that you've done?'

'Nothing,' said Jez. It sounded lame, even to him.

'Then you won't mind if I call in work teams to look over the Tower complex.'

'No!' cried Suzy and Jez together.

'I see,' said Goodman. 'Right. Come with me.' He grabbed Suzy's arm and pulled her out of the office, then marched her off up the darkened corridor.

'Leave her alone!' shouted Jez, but Goodman ignored him. Jez followed. Goodman kept going, through into the PR department, then pushed Suzy into the demo centre, turning to lock the doors behind them, barring the way to Jez.

Jez pushed and pulled at the doors but they were firmly locked. The doors had thick glass windows set into them, and Jez peered through. Goodman had turned on the lights and was at the control panel for the demo tank, then returned to grab Suzy. He pulled her towards him, lifted her and dropped her into the tank with a splash and a howl from Suzy. Goodman leaned over to grab her arm as she spluttered in the tank.

'Now then,' Goodman shouted at Jez, 'I've set the timer there, so you haven't got long. If you don't want a solidified girlfriend, you'll tell me now what you're up to.'

'We'll tell you,' screamed Jez. 'Just let her go.'

'Go on then, tell me.'

'We've evacuated the site because we're going to nullify the phase change at the Tower.'

'How?'

'I don't know!'

'Don't give me that!'

'I don't *know*, I tell you! Suzy, tell him!'

Goodman ignored Suzy and kept looking at Jez. 'Well that's rather unfortunate for your friend here.'

Jez pounded frantically at the doors, but they were solidly built. He took a run at them to batter them in with a shoulder charge but rebounded with a grunt. He looked around. There was nothing to pound them with: no furniture, nothing to break the glass. Glass ...

He ran to the next door up the corridor, and tried it. It opened. The control room, with the large glass window overlooking the main demo tank hall. Jez ran straight through the side door and into the hall. Goodman was nowhere to be seen, and Suzy was pulling herself out of the tank. A red light on the control panel was flashing.

Suzy saw him and shouted something, but simultaneously Jez was knocked off his feet sideways. Goodman. Jez wriggled to one side as Goodman grabbed for him, then scrambled to his feet and ran for Suzy. Goodman was behind him and caught him, and the pair of them careered into the tank and the momentum carried them over the rail. Cold water closed over them and Jez fought for breath. He shook free Goodman's grip on his arm as they both floundered in the water. Suzy was leaning over the rail, grabbing for Goodman's flailing arms. It gave Jez the chance to heave himself out of the tank. He heard

Suzy yell as Goodman caught hold of her. She was being dragged into the tank …

Jez leapt for the control console, but as he did so, the red light stopped flashing. He heard a scream behind him and then silence. Suzy had been released and had fallen backwards against the wall. She had her hands to her mouth, and her eyes were wide. Jez forced himself to look at the tank. A hand was caught half in, half out of an otherwise featureless block of grey solid water.

* * * * *

An hour later they stood at the railing of the pier, looking out to the east. The coast was a braid of light against a darkening sky. Jez looked across at Suzy: the wind was ruffling her hair as she gazed out at the Nuland Tower compound a couple of miles away over the black water. The next day the repercussions would start, but meanwhile the evening had one further event yet to play out.

'Now what happens?' he asked.

'We wait. It won't be long.'

'Are you sure this will work?'

But she just stared out to sea, put a finger to her lips, then put an arm round his waist. He trusted her. It felt wonderful.

Presently she seemed to sniff the air, and looked away from the coast, out to sea. He followed her gaze, and saw…nothing. A trick of the twilight. And yet …Yes, there were low grey mounds in the water, immense, four or five, and more came, in a huge curving arc facing the coast. Suzy glanced up at him, then back at the silent motion in the water. Everything seemed to still, like an orchestra waiting for a conductor's signal to start.

There was a deep sound, no, a vibration - *something*, that churned his stomach and jarred his teeth.

'What is it?' he asked, starting to look around wildly.

'It's all right, it's focussed, we'll only get mild effects here.' She pointed to the towers and said, 'Look.'

There was another rumbling, felt rather then heard, and Nuland Tower seemed to shimmer. Then slowly, very slowly, but now unmistakably, it was moving. Jez stood transfixed as the tower sank, crumbling as it fell, and he saw his career and the last vestiges of the shell he had built up falling too, into a cloud of dust and spray which spread over the waters, and as that thinned, merely the sea, the liquid sea.

He turned to Suzy's smiling face and her eyes, her liquid eyes.

Déjà -Vu

Christopher Enby

David Alexander had a déjà vu in his Brighton flat on the evening of April 12th. Déjà vus are not so very uncommon, and on any other occasion he would have forgotten it by the next day. He was tidying up some of the paperwork that was accumulating in drifts around the place. The trouble with working from home, as he never tired of telling people, was that you never left the bloody office. David's business was stranded between the persistent ideal of the paperless office and the glaring reality of his present situation. He had ziggurats of paperwork crying out for attention. Most personal filing systems are stable to begin with, then gradually acquire a kind of chaotic consciousness and pass beyond the control of their creator. David ran a leaflet distribution company, which made everything worse to the *n*th power.

The clock on the wall said 9.27. The evening news would be almost over, but he turned on the TV anyway to catch the closing headlines. As he moved towards the kitchen to make coffee, he heard the end of an obituary item.

'...that there was nothing left for him to say with his films anyway.'

David wheeled round in time to catch the merest glimpse of a face displayed behind the newsreader's head. Was it Kominski? Damn! Was it? Suddenly a car screeched on the Kingsway outside. The reporter's voice, a glimpse of a face on the screen, the sound of tires - hadn't all this already happened? Didn't he have a dream about this? When? Last night or six months ago? He recognised this moment, this sensation. Déjà vu; just that weird déjà -vu thing. He hadn't had one for ages. Not that he could be certain - he forgot them pretty quickly. There was no more to the item. The newsreader said goodnight, and soon there was a woman in a pink suit telling him what the weather had been like today. Had it been Kominski? Watch the ten o'clock and see if they say anything, he thought. Otherwise, buy a paper in the morning.

There was nothing on the later news, but there was an obituary in the paper. Robert Kominski, Polish film-maker based in Switzerland; auteur director of *Pity, The Fall of Night, The Polish Rider* and recently a trilogy set in the shipyards of his native Gdansk: *Solidarity, Changing Times* and *The Return.* A notoriously reclusive figure, who rarely discussed his films, and never promoted them, Kominski had not worked for over two years since abandoning his last project, a film about the Holocaust which he had finally decided was unfilmable. He had, it was widely rumoured, suffered some kind of breakdown in the face of this project, perhaps as a result of the research he had conducted. He consigned a year's work to the scrapheap and claimed there was nothing for him to say;

he had found the limits of his abilities, and found them wanting.

David folded the paper and rolled it. Looking out from the awning of the newsagent he became aware what a beautiful day it was, even by Brighton's standards. Ten o'clock; time to go.

He walked into the café just off Seven Dials to find Clare already seated and picking dried plaster of Paris from her fingers. They met in the Saucy Sausage every Saturday morning to catch up and pass a couple of hours together. Clare poked strands of russet hair behind her ears and said: 'You know that Polish director who did that film about that artist who went mad?'

'The Polish Rider. Kominski.'

'That's it. I was thinking Kerim Bey. God knows why. Anyway...'

'Hang on; Kerim Bey. What's that from?'

'He's the Turkish guy in *From Russia With Love*, actually. That's why I knew it couldn't be right. Anyway Koszinski –'

'Kominski.'

'- Kominski - died yesterday.'

'I know, I saw the end of a bit on the news, and it's in here as well. You know what we should do? We should all get out one of his films one night and watch it wearing black armbands.'

'I knew you'd say something like that, I just knew it.'

There was a moment of silent grinning, as she waited to see what he'd say.

'Well, at the risk of sounding predictable, I'm glad to be so predictable. Funnily enough, I had a déjà vu last night when I heard about Kominski on the telly. I just caught the end of the report, and then this car skidded right outside the flat and I went Wooo! Wooo! Déjà - vu!'

'When was this?'

'At the end of the news; about half nine.'

'Hmmm. Well, I wasn't watching the news, but I had a déjà vu around then. Funny you mention it, because I'd already forgotten.'

'You didn't hear about Kominski on the news?'

'Yeah, but on the earlier news. At nine thirty I was walking over to Jim's place with Ben. I suddenly thought *I bet we both came out without keys, and we've locked ourselves out*; and I said to Ben er, you have got your keys? And he said 'Who me?' you know, the way he does, and he says, 'You shut the door, Missus. Haven't you got them?' Well, I checked, and I hadn't because I'd changed coats, and he said 'Well isn't it lucky that one of us has half a brain?' Then –'

'You have a whole brain, of course'

'Quite, and erm, that was it. When I checked my pockets I thought, *oh shit I've seen this, and I haven't got any keys*. But you know how you sort of get the sensation after the event, or slightly? So I think I already knew my pocket was empty when the thought occurred to me.'

'You had a déjà vu at exactly the same time as me? What are the chances?'

'Well yours was probably because you knew he was going to die anyway. You did, didn't you? I remember you saying.'

'I knew he was ill.'

'So when you heard he'd died, even just a clue that he'd died, like a fragment, you probably felt you already knew it, you'd convinced yourself you'd already heard it before somewhere. I get that all the time listening to stuff on the radio when I'm working. I find I'm thinking about something, and I realise it's what they're talking about on *Afternoon Forum* or whatever. Maybe you just hear the start of a piece, and your mind subconsciously sort of wanders off, almost unaware of what sparked it.'

David's gaze flickered over the ceiling of the cafe, and over the posters on the walls advertising the usual meditation classes, retro clubs and lost cats. Half-obscured by the festoons of spider plants there was a flyer for Clare's forthcoming sculpture exhibition.

'Still doesn't explain why you had one at exactly the same time,' he said, just a little uneasy about the déjà vu coincidence.

'Perhaps we're psychic.'

'Perhaps I'll get some more teas.'

He would be seeing Clare, along with Ben and couple of others in the evening. Without really planning to, for the rest of that otherwise typical Saturday in Brighton, David checked with people to see if they'd had a déjà vu. He asked Jeri in the seafront post office and Kay in the photocopy shop. He rang Tom, who lived on the outskirts of town in Hangleton and Ellen, who lived in Norfolk. Those that could remember had indeed had similar experiences. Ellen had not had a déjà vu as such, but she had stared at a boiling kettle for a moment in a mental limbo before snapping out of it and taking it off the ring.

That evening found him in the Sussex, a large pub near his flat, which strictly speaking was in Hove, not Brighton. Clare and Ben and a bunch of others, mostly old friends from college, had commandeered the big table near the door. They all had their drinks, but David was still waiting for his black pint to settle, so he eavesdropped on two men nearby. One of them, a stocky, crew cut man in a green bomber jacket was dragging on the last millimetres of a cigarette and recalling an incident of the night before. The band was already playing (an almost unrecognisable *Sunshine of Your Love*), and David had to strain to overhear.

'Remember I ducked out last night to make that phone call? Well, I'm coming back and just outside here I see this girl almost get hit by this car. Just about fifty feet along from the door there. Okay, so this car nearly knocks her flat, but this bloke just comes out of the shadows where that little alley goes down to the sea front, pulls her out the way and totally disappears! I was going to mention it last night, but I forgot. Okay, you've got to picture this. I'm walking along, right, and the girl, woman I should say, is coming towards me, walking in the road, don't know why, and this car's coming towards me too, right up behind her. I swear to God it was going to kill her. But like I say, this guy just grabs her out the way. By the time I've got to her she's okay; she's not hurt or anything, and the guy's nowhere. I looked down that alley, and it's pretty dark, but he's not in it. Must've practically run down it. I didn't go down, cause I wasn't that interested, you know. But you can see the sea at the end of it, and he'd've shown up against the water for a sec, but he wasn't there. And you know what the weirdest bit is? I can't remember the car at all. Couldn't tell you a thing about it. The make, the colour, nothing. And that's not me.'

David took his drink over to the table where the others were sitting. That was unquestionably the screech of tires he'd heard the previous evening. If he hadn't turned on the news and been distracted by Kominski, he might have rushed to the window in time to see this stranger who saved the woman's life and disappeared.

On Sunday he had nothing planned, so he staved off that Hancockesque Sunday afternoon at home feeling by plotting all the déjà -vus on a map of the town. Two other people had had them at exactly the same time as him: Jeri in the post office over the road ('Just at the end of the main news'), and Carl two streets along ('Yeah, when that Polish guy was on the news. I was holding my coffee, and I couldn't remember for a moment whether I was putting it down or picking it up. I still don't know. And you had the same thing. Weird. Maybe we're psychic or something.')

Clare, who lived with Ben a mile and a half away near Preston Park, could be very specific, because Ben was always absolutely on time for appointments. They'd gone to meet their old flatmate at nine-thirty, and his house was two minutes' walk at their speed, so they would have been on the front step at twenty-eight minutes past. This incredible punctuality was something of a standing joke. You really could set your watch by Ben. Tom in Hangleton was slightly further out, maybe two miles. At nine-thirty he was definitely setting the video for some old musical on satellite TV. Thinking back, he had moved to press *record* after loading the tape, only to find he'd already done it. Was this a déjà vu? At the time he'd just felt surprise at how setting the video had become a series of conditioned reflexes. But it was certainly at fractionally before nine-thirty, because he would not have taped the commercials if he could have helped it. The only person David had contacted in London, fifty miles away, had been smoking certain home-made cigarettes more or less constantly since getting in from work at six. She had no idea what she was doing at exactly half past nine, and what kind of weirdo question was this anyway?

David looked at the map. It was pointless trying to work out if there was a clustering of odd experiences in Brighton. Most of the people he had spoken to were in Brighton, so the results would obviously be biased. With a start he realised no one had had an experience earlier than him. In fact it was obvious now he looked that they were slightly later the further they were from him. Ellen's was definitely the latest, because she missed the first few minutes of the local news while making coffee. Nine thirty-one or two at least. Out of curiosity he put a cross over his house and drew concentric rings around it. It worked. Even with some allowance for human error each occurrence of déjà vu was later the further it was from his flat. Ellen's result sat all alone up in Norfolk. He hauled out a bigger map. Next to Brighton he wrote 9.27 - 9.30. Next to Ellen in Norfolk he wrote 9.31(?) Should he call Jane in Edinburgh? They'd been out of touch for the last month or two at least. Curiosity overwhelmed him. He rang; they talked and at the end he asked, 'By the way, did you have déjà vu last night, about nine-thirty?'

'What?'

'Did you have a déjà vu last night at around nine-thirty? Ish?'

'Just a minute.' She put a hand over the mouthpiece and conferred with someone else in the room. A moment later she came back on. 'You really want to know?'

'I really want to know.'

'At nine-thirty last night, or somewhere around there anyway, we were trying to remember the name of that film by that Polish director who died. It was on the news. He did that film about the painter who killed his...daughter, was it?'

'The Polish Rider.'

'Right. We saw it in the paper today. None of us could remember it. We were all sitting around vegging, I guess.'

'This was just after you saw him on the news?'

'Yes, we were talking over the local news, waiting for the weather. And none of us could remember that fucking film title, and we'd all bloody seen it! It was at the Filmhouse about six months ago.'

'But this was a collective lapse of memory, not a déjà -vu?'

'No, not a déjà vu. Why?'

So Jane and her friends had probably been slightly later still. The evidence seemed pretty convincing. Déjà vus or at least some kind of mental lapses had been spreading out from the middle of Brighton like ripples on a pond when a stone has been thrown in. This was all crazy, of course: a classic example of distorting data to prove some ridiculous point. Outside it was bright and inviting. David threw down the pencil and walked out into the afternoon.

He walked along the sea front, passed by whizzing bicycles and lolloping dogs. It hardly seemed like April - Summer seemed to have arrived early. Presently he found himself in the arcade below the Palace Pier. He had little time for most of these ear-splitting games, least of all for the kind that pretended you were going to win lots of money on them at almost no cost to yourself. The arcade was buzzing with tourists and kids spending, spending, spending and screeching at each other. What on earth was he doing here anyway? Over the milling hordes of crop-headed children he saw the old *Star Wars* game, a climb-inside-and-pretend-to-be-a-pilot game for which he had a lingering childhood attachment. With what now seemed endearingly simple graphics, you were supposed to shoot down squads of TIE fighters, blow the tops off an assortment of towers and finally race down a long trench to fire your torpedoes into an exhaust port and blow up the dreaded Death Star, all the while avoiding countless energy bolts which would knock out your force shields, like a cat losing its lives.

He was, he knew, absolutely rubbish at this sort of thing. He had the reflexes for it, but was unwilling to put in the required practice. It all seemed too trivial. Yet without really knowing why, he put his coins in the slot and settled into the seat. TIE fighters circled and dived, dropping their sparkly little bombs, forcing him to dodge and weave when he could not shoot them all. Suddenly they were gone, and he was flying low over the surface of the space station, taking pot shots at towers and bunkers, dodging all the shots aimed at him to the accompaniment of rather muffled little bangs and pops. And then he was in the trench for the final run. He shot out gun emplacements, and snuck under and over barriers, all the while looking for the exhaust port that would yield him a big bonus and a new game. He became distracted by the thought that the graphics of the game, though primitive, were actually better than the ones the rebels had had in their x-wing fighters in the film. Up ahead the exhaust port came into view. He used the Force, pressed the firing controls on the steering wheel, and missed.

There was a crunch of metal and an Artoo-Deetoo squawk from the speakers, and before he knew what was happening, he was back at the start of the trench again, dodging barriers. The game had rewound like a tape, putting him back in the past for another try. Surely he had been here before? Déjà …

He scrambled out of the machine and ran out onto the pebbly beach. He wanted so much to shout to the skies, to holler at the gleaming white pier above him but he remembered he was an Englishman, and instead he scuffed up some stones and said 'eureka' under his breath. That was it. That was bloody it! Get away from all this noise and bustle and think it out clearly. Up ahead the sun was dropping low in the sky, and shone straight into his eyes. He'd forgotten to bring any sunglasses and would just have to put up with the discomfort. It would be easier to think with half closed eyes anyway.

'Okay then,' he said half aloud, 'you had a strange disorientating jolt when you messed up in the last seconds of the game, when the machine effectively rolled back time to give you a second attempt. Just for a second, a split-second, it was like déjà vu. No warning; no little message saying 'Bad luck! Try again!' Just an instant return to an earlier point in time, to the beginning of the trench. What if –' he was raising his voice now, '- just what if someone had the means to turn time back for real; to cancel out a stupid mistake, and go back to a point earlier on when it would be possible to effect a better outcome? That woman, whoever she was, and whatever she was doing, was going to be hit by that car outside my flat. She should have been injured or dead; but a mysterious someone who came and went without being seen properly saved her. He got her out the way, and saved her life. He adjusted time; rolled it back, and disappeared. So a new future unrolls for all of us. God knows what happened to the old one in which the girl dies, but this is the one we're in now. And we know, or at least I know, that this intervention in time has occurred, because everyone in the area experienced some sort of temporal confusion, like we were living that last second again. What about Ellen and Jane? Hmm. Maybe the ripple gets fainter and fainter as it spreads. Or maybe that business of forgetting a name, of staring into space for a moment, or standing at the top of the stairs wondering why you went up there, maybe all these things are what happens when two ripples cross over each other. If these alterations happen all over the world the ripples obviously have to intersect here and there. Maybe the time-adjusting people pulled somebody away from a car in Boston or somewhere, or pushed him under one just as likely, and the ripple came over the sea to us. God, what am I saying! This is insane!'

But it was a great story. David had often been called a conspiracy theorist. His response was that at least he did theorise, which was a sign of a brain at least half-working. Anyway, he knew for a fact that all the really big conspiracy theories were dreamed up by these guys from the CIA and FBI in smoke-filled rooms. Then the theories were subtly and quietly released into the world to divert attention from the real issues. You had to hand it to these secret service people.

A month later, David had a tidy collection of rejection slips from every newspaper and magazine he could think of. 'Facetious' they said, and 'hysterical.' 'Science fiction' and 'untenable.' The battered manuscript sat on the corner of his cluttered desk in disgrace. The title page, bearing the legend 'Interferences In Time - A new theory of déjà vu by David Alexander' was dog-eared and had come loose, giving his essay a shabby, rejected look. What a load of crap. It had been a pretty stupid idea; that was obvious now.

Another month passed, and David was at a private view of Clare's sculpture. He was introduced to Nick Muzyka, a freelance reporter. Somehow they got around to the subject of Polish spellings - sometimes four consonants in a row, maybe one vowel in an eight-letter name.

'Actually it was a Pole who sent me off on the weirdest train of thought back in April,' said David. 'You know Kominski, the film director? When he died I had a déjà vu as I heard about it, and at the same time this car skidded outside my house. I convinced myself eventually that the skid was an important event, which had been changed by these people who can alter history to suit their own ends, but there's always a tiny little time lag of a half-second or whatever, and that's déjà vu.'

'What a corker! You should publish it; but I wonder...I just have this weird feeling I've heard this before somewhere...Tell you what, I know the science editor of the Observer. They're just about to print a series of articles I've done on computers in schools. I'll tell her to take a look at this idea, okay? Remind me to give you her number. It's in my coat, I'll get it to you when I leave, which might as well be now; I notice they've run out of white.'

* * * * *

Resnais Corporation.
Time Adjustment Division.
Adjustment Report. Filed by Operative 16309.

Subject under observation, David Alexander, attempted to reveal truth of déjà vu. Subject was able, by combination of chance and unscientific research to form a theory of time adjustment and localised ripple effect. Long term consequences of his actions have been assessed and an amendment to history effected forthwith. Chosen point of intervention was 11.17.51/13/4/96. Subject's friend Clare Jacquard was not heard to say the words 'I knew you'd say something like that. I just knew it.' David Alexander was not reminded of his déjà vu experience of previous night, and incident will never arise again. Subject will not formulate theory, nor will he ever consider déjà vu to be other than it appears: a simple slip of the mind. His pursuit of the mystery, committal of discoveries to paper and subsequent publication of article in Observer Newspaper have all, along with related temporal incidents, been shunted off into parallel time, where such events can have no effect on the progress of THE GREAT PLAN.

What the Butler Saw

Veronica Williams

Early morning mist hangs in ectoplasmic swathes across the facades of hotels, guest houses, made-over Regency bow fronts and slabs of concrete flats stained by salt and weather, rising like rows of old teeth along the sea front. Here and there a window glitters where the rising sun tries to peer in at the panes. The incoming tide gnaws at the shingle, sucks it, and spits it out at the bare, blue-with-cold feet of Darcy Drumm.

Darcy is long and thin and pallid, like something grown in a cellar. His bony shoulders hunch against the chill air, his knees cling together; his narrow face wears an expression of mixed distaste for the task ahead, and determination to get it over with. He carries his clothes in a plastic bag. He is a most unlikely bather-to-be, shivering on the deserted beach on a September morning.

In the gaunt shade of the landwards portion of the Pier, it is quite cold. The slop and slap of the tide echoes around the corroded, weed-fringed iron pillars and bounces up to what is left of the decking; debris curdles around these pillars ready to be stranded on the beach when the sea is tired of playing with it. Darcy makes a face of loathing, as he thinks of sewage and septicaemia, but, perching his bag upon his head, he advances into the water. First his knees and then his hips are engulfed; the waves, cold and alien, rise to his chest and Darcy makes thin whistlings of distress as he loses touch with his body under water, but he wades on resolutely towards the seaward end of the Pier, long since cut off.

From a distance, the Pier resembles a broken-backed insect, tottering out to sea on many shambly legs, some of them missing where part of the structure collapsed, its head the island of buildings - theatre, tea rooms, shelters and kiosks - derelict and long abandoned. Down below, wicked little eddies spin to and fro around the iron legs; a long piece of lavatory paper undulates past Darcy, a sea-serpent heading for the shore. In the gloom beneath the decking, where the sun is too early to penetrate, the air is dank and strong and dreadful, ripe enough to shrivel the nostrils, but now Darcy is afloat, hauling himself along on the struts that link the pillars, and he has seen the first of a series of ladders, has seized the nearest rung and is swarming up, up, clutching his bag in his teeth. He half-expects to be hailed from the beach by police or an early bather, but still no-one is about, though the sun has sucked up the mist, revealing cliffs of architecture and native chalk stretching away into the east, white above the dancing sparkle of the waves.

Darcy drags himself from rung to rung, rust rasping his blue hands. He is not athletic and his hoarse breathing sends echoes to join those that roam to and fro under the decking, but now he has achieved the topmost rung and his eyes water in sunshine as he clambers through a trapdoor, its lid long rotted away. Wheezing now with strain, Darcy collapses on to weather bleached boards and lies flat, a long pale rag laid out to dry.

He thinks that his employer, Lockshott, ought to be grateful to him, but knows all too well that Lockshott never shows or feels gratitude, believing that because he pays rather more than well, that should be sufficient reward.

'Do not attempt to remove the machine,' Lockshott has instructed him. 'Just make sure that it is still there, and leave the rest to me.'

A vast burnished desert of desktop lies between Darcy, standing, and Lockshott, seated. Darcy sees Lockshott reflected upside down, his thick fingers tapping their images in the polished wood. Darcy says

'Yes, Mr Lockshott,' dutifully.

'I believe in settling problems legally,' says Lockshott, who believes no such thing, 'but these oafs on the local council force me to act. Since they have never even answered my letters, why should I offer to buy the slot machine?'

Darcy murmurs a reply that might be anything.

'I want your report ASAP, Drumm, so get on with it.' Darcy turns to leave, but Lockshott's suety countenance cracks into a small grin. 'Here, take this.' And he slides a gleaming coin across the desk. Darcy swoops and grabs it and Lockshott nods approval of the swift reaction. It is a meagre nod, no effort wasted. 'Use it and report to me if the machine is still working, will you? You may find out just what it was that the butler saw.'

Darcy wonders why Lockshott wants yet another gadget to add to the hundreds that fill the mansion in Surrey, the town house in London, the castle in Scotland and half a dozen other residences in as many countries. Darcy owns very little; he dislikes clutter.

Now, lying on the boards, he takes the coin out of a pocket in his shorts. A shining old penny, brighter than the sun; George the Fifth still reigns. But Darcy thinks it very unlikely that even this venerable coin will activate the slot machine. The storms of a decade have battered the Pier with all the wild energy of Channel weather, tearing and scouring it, and if the machine still exists, which Darcy doubts, rust will have eroded it; salt will have eaten its inner workings.

The complex of pleasure buildings that looms over Darcy bear witness to those years of neglect; the great grandiose structure and its siblings on a smaller scale look as if a good shove would flatten them. He replaces the coin and, dragging the bag of clothes, begins to inch his way to where he can stand without being seen from the shore. At once it becomes apparent that the boards bristle with splinters and are encrusted with enough gull-guano to stock all the garden centres in Sussex. A rank stench rises up to assault Darcy's nostrils and he feels like a martyr to Lockshott's collector's greed as he stands up in the shelter of a kiosk that projects from the crumbling bulk of the main building and is able to pick splinters out of his goose-flesh and pull on the grey hooded sweatshirt and jogging-bottom, hoping that thus clad he will merge into his surroundings. If the police appear, Darcy knows that it will be useless to invoke Lockshott's protection; the man loathes and fears publicity so profoundly that even a hint of it produces quite alarming reactions, and Darcy has no wish to become their target.

He has a story all ready. Too much to drink the night before in too many pubs - no, of course he wasn't driving - a bet made with a character whose name he has forgotten...who can prove or disprove it?

The morning air is sharp but Darcy is warming up nicely. He leaps up and down, whacking his arms across his chest, but imagines that the boards beneath him begin to tremble, and hastily moves away until he is hidden from the shore. A quick glance over his shoulder shows him that the sea front now seems to be a very long way off, curiously unreal and as flat as a stage backcloth. Darcy has a distinct and disquieting impression that the land has begun to recede into the northern distances. Feeling a little seasick, he transfers his attention to the buildings of the Pier.

They are a sorry sight: paint has peeled, wood is blistered and rotten, all the framework has warped badly. An atmosphere of decaying despair breathes from it and Darcy suspects much of the interior has fallen into the sea. Unpleasant vibrations tickle the soles of his feet. On the very end of the Pier, there is a narrow walk or veranda that was once glassed in, from which trippers could kid themselves that they were able to see France. The sea appears at once to be very near and very far off, as successions of waves advance and surge shorewards. Shielding his eyes against the rising sun's glare, Darcy sees the object of Lockshott's desire, a waist-high post of cast iron supporting an eye-piece. It may once have been bright crimson, but has faded to the sickly tint of boiled liver. Darcy can just decipher the words 'WHAT THE BUTLER SAW' above a slot for pennies.

He feels great relief at not having to admit failure to Lockshott, who treats failure as if it is a personal insult. All Darcy has to do now is to go ashore and report. But the incoming tide has flowed in faster than he anticipated and the sea is very deep and dark and, he guesses, numbingly cold. He cringes at the prospect of lowering himself into those obsidian depths. He is no swimmer. If he waits until the tide ebbs to its lowest point, return will be easy. In the meantime (he thinks vaguely that this may take some hours) he may as well use Lockshott's penny; at least he can say that he tried.

A bigger wave than its fellows rushes towards the beach, twanging the Pier's supports like harp strings. Darcy starts nervously; the Pier might almost be marching out to sea. Gratefully, he clings to the slot machine; it is very firm and solid. Somewhere a loose door or plank claps like a gunshot, and he fumbles the coin into the slot, hears it clink down into the works; the eyepiece presses hard against his forehead and he smells rust and salt and old metal as events begin to unfold in flickerings, jerks, and faded sepia. They should, by now, be mildly comic, but Darcy finds them disturbing, and is unable to withdraw.

After a title - again, 'WHAT THE BUTLER SAW', executed in elaborate flourishes - a scene appears: a landing or anteroom, an ancestral portrait on striped wall paper, a chair, an aspidistra upon a tall stand. The butler enters, bald and black clad, posturing like Figaro in a badly produced opera, and tip-toes with exaggerated caution towards a door painted upon the side wall. He withdraws, advances again with forefinger upon his lips, and stoops to apply his eye to the keyhole. Starting back, he registers great dismay; clearly he belongs to the Henry Irving school of acting. Darcy mutters

'Corny!'

Slowly, the scene changes to a bedroom. More striped wall paper, a large brass bed, tumbled sheets. On these sits a young woman, with awkward insouciance; she is amply endowed with bosom, hair and thighs. She removes a stocking and twirls her garter, invitingly, on a forefinger; her underclothes are at once revealing, yet voluminous. With a dreadful smirk, she allows a shoulderstrap to slide down her rounded arm, and her lips pout, plumply, in promise. At the end of the bed stands a young man with a fiercely pointed moustache; he holds his trousers at arms' length, like a signal.

The girl leans forward, still twirling her garter, and her chemise falls to expose a bosom of voluptuous dimensions; her partner becomes almost cross-eyed with lust. However, before any further developments the scene changes to show the butler fairly hopping about in a frenzy, his face contorted in mock horror...and his features, his gestures, swell to become as large as life in Darcy's sight. Larger still, as if he stares out at Darcy staring in...and Darcy is pulled, unbearably stretched, elongated like a rubber band...

Like the band released, he shoots forward into the machine. It is a terrifying experience, and exceedingly painful. Bone-wracked and breathless, Darcy is spat forth into the machine, to land on hands and knees at the butler's feet. Both are too stunned by this turn of events to speak, but then, while Darcy wheezes and whimpers, the butler rushes past him and takes a running dive at the place from which Darcy has come...and vanishes.

Darcy struggles to his feet. The painted door bursts open and the younger participant in the drama leaps through the gap, bawling

'Wait for me, Jack!' and follows the butler, still clutching his trousers, which blow out behind him like a bizarre banner. As he too disappears through the wall, Darcy blunders after him, goaded into desperation. But the wall is now solid, there is no aperture to be seen or felt. Half stunned by his impact upon it, Darcy slips to the floor and a firmament of stars blind his vision until trickles of water clear it and he finds the young woman beside him, bathing his forehead from a wash-stand jug. Her voice as piercingly shrill as a gnat's, tortures his ears.

'That a bit better, ducky?'

Darcy stares wildly around him. He sees the striped paper, the portrait, the aspidistra, and the anxious face, none too clean, of the girl, and he mutters obscenities.

'Thass right, ducky,' the girl says. 'You got stuck in here, same as me. Ooh, I could kill that Jack! An' Fred! They could've taken me with 'em, the brutes!'

'What do you mean, stuck?' The sordid room reels around Darcy; the girl helps him into the bedroom and he slumps on the bed. Its springs jangle suggestively but Darcy can only lie there while the awful, the impossible truth steals into his awareness. The girl flops down beside him.

'See, we was told it was a film job. The money wasn't bad an' Jack an' me 'ad been resting for a bit, so we thought it might bring in a bob or two if they took us on for some more, see? Gotta eat 'aven't yer? Fred did the managin' bit, said they'd easy polish us off in a mornin'.' Tears flow down her plump cheeks. 'Oh ha, ever so bloody ha! I dunno what went wrong but it polished us off good and proper, stuck in this mucky hole fer Gawd knows 'ow long an' now they've got out, blast their bloody eyes, an' I'm still here!'

She weeps loudly and copiously, tears washing clean tracks on her grubby face. Darcy sees that nothing is clean here; all is filmed over with grime and there is a close, fetid smell. He pushes a handful of sheet into the girl's hand, not daring to speculate how long she and her fellow actors have been trapped within the slot machine, or why no-one ever released them before Lockshott's penny did so. Are there, perhaps, dozens of lost voyeurs stuck somewhere in the recesses of the machinery, unable to free themselves?

He does know that Lockshott never gives up, and sooner or later, infuriated by Darcy's silence, he will resort to action...but lethargy overcomes him; he is unable to move so much as an eyelash, and the girl's voice reaches him from far away.

'The bloody...penny's...run...out...'

Darcy thinks that when Lockshott puts in another coin, he is going to get one hell of a shock...and then he and the girl sink into suspended animation…but not into total oblivion.

Darcy's stifled and paralysed self still holds awareness. He cannot reason, but he does hear, and his inert body experiences tremors, reverberations beneath and around him, that may be the rush of waves surging inland, or winds that sight, breathe, hurl their invisible pressures against the Pier's structure. Or a swinging door that slams, or a gull alighting, or furtive footfalls light as dust.

Darcy knows when a muffled murmur of voices comes to him from the outside world, and his surroundings shake to the jar of crowbars and the slot-machine is prised loose from the deck of the Pier. He is aware that it is being raised, tilting and surging alarmingly, though no change of level affects the bedroom or the bed; he and the girl still lie motionless. But there is evident activity, and noise as a trolley rumbles over the boards, before the scene of the butler's eavesdropping is manhandled into a van. The hum of its engine tells Darcy that he, still captive, is on the way to somewhere.

What he does not know is that Lockshott, frustrated by the absence of news from his assistant, has taken the law into his own hands. Lockshott considers that theft is an ugly word; he prefers Rescue Part of Our Heritage From Neglect, and if anyone questions the activities of a small group of workmen on the Pier, Lockshott can provide answers. Besides, he knows that no-one really looks at workmen as long as they appear to be genuine and seem to know what they are doing.

Events run in reverse as the slot machine is unloaded and heaved onto another trolley. Then, after so much movement, comes silence, uneasily prolonged. No more voices of waves or winds. For all Darcy knows, his prison has been dumped at the local tip.

Then his hearing is assaulted so violently that a shock of mega-proportions shatters the limbo in which he is trapped. Huge, clangourous gongings reverberate deafeningly to and fro, trailing metallic echoes in surge after surge through his body. Darcy is not exactly electrified into activity, but he does sit up, and the jangle of bedsprings, like an out of tune piano, tells him that his companion has bounced to her feet and is tugging at him. Her face is wild and hopeful.

'Get up, do! Someone's put a penny in!'

Darcy needs no urging. A frantic desire to escape propels him from the bed to the anteroom, leaping over the aspidistra which has crashed from its stand to lie amid broken pottery on the floor. He makes a rush, a running dive, at the slot machine's eyepiece, but is brought up short by an alarming sight: a magnified eye like a grey poached egg, glaring in at him.

Darcy knows that eye, and his knees turn to spaghetti. Lockshott has inserted a bright new penny in the slot machine. The eyes is his, and it is clear that he (shaken to the core for once in his life) has identified his missing henchman, lurking within Lockshott's precious loot. Lockshott is visibly enraged, and Darcy quails.

Only for an instant does he cringe. The girl gives him such a sharply imperious shove in the back that Darcy is sent flying forwards and, stretched like chewing gum, hurtles through the eyepiece to land on hands and knees in the real world of Lockshott's vast store-room. Lockshott barely manages to avoid being knocked down; his bellow of fury and dismay galvanises Darcy into leaping up and bolting with acceleration powered by terror, through a nearby open door.

Behind him the girl screeches

'Aow! I've tore me drawers!' but she dodges Lockshott (still reeling from the assault on his dignity) and manages to race past Darcy as they emerge into the hot, salty sunlight. They run at astonishing speed across an expanse of grass, spurred on by the uproar of pursuit in the rear. But the merciless, burning sunlight works a terrible transformation upon the two fleeing figures. Darcy sees his companion becoming strangely insubstantial, disintegrating as she runs; the glare of light upon her robust contours causes them to shrivel to shreds and tatters of degrading celluloid. His own bony hands lose their strength and with a soundless shriek of horror Darcy sees that he too is falling apart, his bodily substance withered to nothing and scattered by the sea-wind. When Lockshott reaches the spot, there is only a little, brittle dust lying upon the grass.

The Digger at the Dyke

Peter T Garratt

Mary Cecilia meant to take her last journey to the Devil's Dyke on the bus. Since her early days in Brighton, as she first heard the dreaded cry of 'Next' when she'd only been auditioning to be an extra, there'd been a song in her head which began: 'Mary Cecilia Bruin/ Went from town on the Burgess Hill Bus'. It would describe the way she planned to end her long but unstarry career by jumping off the second or third letter 'O' of the HOVE WOODS sign on the Dyke, the great hill which superstitious locals still called the work of the Devil. Mary Cecilia had no choice but to go there now, if it meant meeting the Devil himself.

She could walk there and save the bus fare money. She would need it that evening for a bag of chips if she again bottled out of the Great Leap Forward.

She decided to walk. It was just dawn, Midsummer's Day. The stones on the beach and the weird calls of the gulls had woken her long before the first bus.

Something smelled vile. Probably it was her. She had spent the last two nights and the intervening day fermenting her decision in cheap cider. She hadn't washed herself or her sleeping bag for ages, but there was something worse... she was above high water mark where the tide couldn't disguise the use dogs and birds made of the shingle.

She crawled out of the sleeping bag, found her flip-flops, and staggered to her feet. She felt more hung over than a stag after the night of a Hunt Ball, but she had an irrational urge to look and smell her best. Last time she had tried to make the leap, people had stood on the bus to the Dyke rather than sit next to her. She had remembered her mother's injunctions about the condition she and her underwear needed to be in in the event of an accident and bottled out completely, bar-crawling shame-faced back to the flat. It had been her condition that evening that led her landlord to order her out.

She made for the sea, pulling off her clothes. The other failed actors with whom she shared the beach wouldn't notice. 'Let me not live,' she prayed. 'To lie on the stones in the morning and not even wake up.' She would plunge into the sea naked, like whatever remote ancestor had once pointlessly crawled out of it. It would have been better if her ancestors had remained in the sea and become dolphins, or even fish.

The tide was out. She kept her flip-flops on till she reached the sand: the narrow strip at the very edge of the sea that only appeared at low tide. She had never learned to walk the shingle of Brighton Beach even now she lived on it. When she had been new to the town and bright and confident every morning, she had landed a part in the pilot episode of Brightwatch. However, though she had looked pretty good on the beach in those days, her feet had let her down. Hopping down the accursed heap of rocks with an expression like a victim in a Turkish jail drama while an unfortunate swimmer drowned slowly hadn't been in the contract. She was never seen on screen in the famous amber swimsuit except for a sequence in which she had been bending over, and any watching casting directors could see the whole of her superb but anonymous behind and nothing identifiable of her face.

She kicked off her flip-flops and strode across the damp sand to the water, where her feet were almost as badly affected by the cold as they had just been by the pebbles. Still, this wasn't a day to loll on the beach. She splashed on past the ends of the stone breakwaters, only to find the water scarcely reached her knees. The stony area of the beach sloped, which made it harder to go down, but the sand was flat. Her feet were starting to get used to the cold when she realised she was again on stones, sharp ones like empty shells. She recoiled indignantly, staggered, and found herself on a steep slope leading to deeper water. She pitched forward and wound up face down and floundering in deep cold water, salty as hungover tears. She realised she could drown herself here, that if her life flashed before her, it would leave her no incentive to struggle to safety.

Instinct took over. She twisted till her head was uppermost and kicked and push-paddled till it broke the surface. She spat and sneezed the water, but had swallowed none. Her feet found the bottom... it was sandy again, deeper, but she could stand with her head and shoulders above the surface, pale-blonde hair floating around her like spray from a waterfall.

The sea was very calm, and she was starting to feel warmer. The sky to the east was still very pale, scarcely brighter than the lights on the promenade and the piers. She had no idea of the time... it was Midsummer's Day; it would be hours before Brighton awoke. She relaxed into a position, half-standing and half floating, in which she could soak her hair in the water and exchange the filth for salt.

She floated on her back and considered her next move. Pills were out, she was sure her stomach would reject them and puke them up, and there was no chance of her opening her veins. She fainted at the thought of blood and hated it so much that she would sooner live on than see her own. She'd been known to refuse Bloody Marys. She was feeling the cold less, and being in the water was getting quite pleasant. One option would be to backstroke out to sea till her strength gave out and she sank gently into oblivion. Yes, that was it. It would save her the long, painful walk to the Devil's Dyke past the studios and the homes of the stars, past Sharon Stun's great house with its wrought-iron gates.

On the other hand, she had always been a strong swimmer, and one summer at drama school had been a real lifeguard in a municipal pool. She didn't trust herself to not swim back and spend the day exhausted on the shingle. If she did manage to drown, she wondered if anyone would bother to report her missing, if her body would be identified when it washed ashore. If it was, her death would be reported as an accident: 'FAILED BRIGHTWATCH BABE COULDN'T EVEN SAVE HERSELF'. That would never do. She was an actress in a town full of false piety about the quality of the films it made, which had forced her to become a babe and fail at that. Jumping off the HOVE WOODS sign would tell everyone why she had died. Jumping at the Dyke would remind people that the Devil had always been active in the area, and he still was.

She turned over and swam to the beach. She found her flip-flops and tackled the stones. There was salt in her mouth and her skin and hair didn't feel as clean as she'd hoped. She reached the lower prom and hurried to the beach shower. There was no soap or hot water so she just stood as the cold spray ran down her, dissolving the salt. She was flushed from the climb and almost enjoyed it, licking her lips and finally opening her mouth and drinking the water in an effort to re-hydrate from her hangover.

She was feeling cleaner and more purposeful. Of course, she was completely naked, but she was well past caring about that. The days when she had worn a coat with a hood to sneak into the LappyCat Club were well behind her. She didn't suppose anyone would pay to see her nudity now... though looking down, she realised she didn't look as gross as she had a few weeks before, when she could still afford to eat fish and chips twice a day and keep up with the lager drinkers. Vodka and very occasional chips, pointlessly supplemented with the last of her vitamins, had thinned her figure to a faded semblance of its Brightwatch best.

She even thought of going to the Dyke nude, but that wouldn't be practical. She had had the forethought after the last suicide fiasco to wash an appropriate set of clothes, and keep them in a separate compartment of her holdall to her filthy regular things. She hurried back trying to dry off in the air. She noticed an old man in a Glasgow Celtic shirt staring at her as if she was some tawdry sea-nymph, but ignored him. People should expect to see strange things in Brighton.

A few years earlier she had bought a nice imitation leather holdall for projected trips to film festivals and to studios and theatres in America. Unlike everything else she owned, it had not been used often. There was a separate compartment which had kept her best clothes clean. She had included a towel embroidered with 'La Pension Touristique, Cannes', and was able to dry herself properly. There was no underwear but the G-string she had kept from her audition for 'LappyCats the Movie', not the less expensive one she had worn at the club proper. However, the amber 'Brightwatch' T-shirt had been designed to be worn without a bra, and now she had lost weight her implants were doing an adequate job. Next she put on a black leather mini-skirt she had been issued on reaching the final audition for 'Base Instinct'. It was identical to the one Sharon Stun had worn in the movie, and was about as short as it could be and still be defined as a skirt. Lastly, a pair of fairly comfortable scholls, property of a prestigious theatre company which had never paid her any other way. She tipped out the holdall. Only the bag itself was sellable. There was a thin file with her resume and a few clippings, another with the few souvenirs she had kept since reaching Brighton. Everything from her earlier life was in the room her parents kept for her in Chumpton Magna, against the day she would return to take up her true vocation as a typist and start assessing the marriageability of the local estate agents.

She decided to keep the holdall and the two files, a half-used mascara and a thin lipstick pencil, one that outlined her lips rather than coloured them. She stuffed the best of her filthy clothes into her noxious sleeping bag and lugged it to an arch of the Prom, where the homeless had an agreement that nothing not sellable would be stolen. Not that there would be much point coming back for this stuff. She had to face the fact that if she didn't make the leap this time, she would have to go on the game or start shoplifting, two things she had sworn she would never do.

Mary Cecilia was ready for the walk to Devil's Dyke. The sky wasn't much brighter...she had been woken by the False Dawn. Everything was false in Movie Town, she reflected as she clattered up the steps to the Upper Prom. She felt purposeful and almost good. She had her file of reviews of her stage work and her two speaking roles in films. Producers and casting directors would realise, when she died this spectacular death, how false their claims to talent and idealism were. She had planned this walk often.

She reached the Upper Prom opposite the Melrose Fish Restaurant and Movie Museum, the place where the world's first ever public showing of a moving picture had been held, back in the 1890s. Pedants might write magazine articles claiming there had been earlier showings of crude proto-films in London and Paris, but Mary Cecilia did not read obsessive zines. Before turning inland, she glanced up at the blocks of luxury flats that rose behind the hotels and dwarfed them. Mary Cecilia knew that Ali Wooden lived in the penthouse of one of these Manhattan-like towers. She toyed briefly with the idea of breaking in and jumping off the roof. It was a plan she had often considered, but she admired Wooden's independent films, and never claimed they would have been better if she had had bigger roles. That Sharon Stun had first been noticed as 'Stunning Girl on Train' in 'Memories of Stardom' was an irrelevance, though Mary Cecilia had never worked out why her own part as 'Second Girl on Train' had led to nothing. Besides, though she had once applied to be a guide on the 'Homes of the Stars' tourbus, and had done a lot of research, she could never remember which tower was which.

She turned inland, through streets which were still almost dark. Whatever the locals said about Brighton's mystic quality, it was still the brash place where Harry Lagman had set his tacky soap about offshore oil dynasties. It was Hove where the movie pioneers had made their stand and refused to 'Go West'. Without Hove, with its wooded avenues of elegant mansions and the vast movie lots on top of the Downs, the British film industry wouldn't lead Europe, let alone the world. She crossed the invisible border into Hove, the shining city where the world's dreams were made into light; the dark place where all her own dreams had died. She turned up a steep street, beginning the long climb to the Devil's Dyke. Soon she started to tire. The Dyke was the highest point for many miles... that was why the HOVE WOODS sign was at its summit... and she wondered if it was true what the locals said, that the hill was a heap of spoil from a ditch dug by the Devil to flood Sussex and drown the people. As her chest got tighter and the scholls no longer seemed to fit, Mary Cecilia started to believe in the Devil and his works.

There was nothing for it but to push on. She had walked out of the LappyCat Club before the ultimate humiliation of being sacked...she was therefore voluntarily jobless, and it would be weeks before she qualified for the dole. She was voluntarily homeless, because the bored official at the Housing Department had never tried to get past the landlord's dogs, who lived permanently on the stairs to her flat, trained to raise the rafters at the vile smell of her. She could not get a job, because no one wanted a failed LappyCat or an actress who was resting on a stony beach. As for acting, her talent had not been recognised in this accursed town, had never been allowed to develop. No, only the Devil was her friend.

She plodded doggedly for an age, until she reached the Dyke Road proper, then continued on, uphill. The sky was quite bright now, but she could not yet see the sun. Ahead was a big sign, not the HOVE WOODS sign, but the more modest emblem of the world's oldest movie studio, NINETEENTH CENTURY, FOLKS. She reached the main office building. Red-bricked and ivy-clad, it had once been a grammar school, and the backlot behind it playing fields. She reflected that this studio had been making movies for a hundred years, since the days of the Hove Pioneers, and her name had never appeared in the credits of any of them. She hurried on till she came to another unwelcome sight, a high wall, behind which a Victorian house had been fancifully crenellated like a castle. The battlements were made of stone, not cardboard, which was appropriate, for Mary Cecilia knew that it was the home of the most controversial man in film.

Raul Pervhoven had made his name when he turned away from the near-arthouse world of Nineteen CF, and turned his gaze up the hill to the brighter lights of H-Woods. Raul had given her the nearest thing she ever had to a break in his first H-Wood movie, 'We Can Remember it for you Wholesale'. OK, she'd played a mutant, and her costume had consisted mainly of a rubber face mask, but SF fans insisted and even wrote that she had been a good mutant. Alas, no one cared what they wrote. Sharon Stun had not worn a mask: she had second billing after Benny Cranach.

After Raul Pervhoven's castle, the houses got bigger and better fortified. No one who lived up here worked for 19CF or the indies, and they wanted you to know it. Those who didn't have stalkers wanted people to think they did. She paused for a breath where the old shepherd's droveway crossed the Dyke Road. She knew that far away across the valley it was called Preston Drove. Then it became a steep narrow street rising to her present position called simply The Drove. Across the road it continued into Hove proper, and here it was known as Rodeo Drove, the mega-exclusive shopping street of the stars and their hangers-on. The sky was getting very red in the east... it must be nearly sunup. Red sky in the morning, shepherd's warning, she thought. She should never hang around Rodeo Drove, remembering that she had never bought so much as a G-string there. She should do something less depressing, like committing suicide.

After 'Wholesale', the Festival Fringe had offered her the witch in a stage version of 'Trek Macbeth'. They had only been able to afford one witch, and she hadn't been paid, apart from keep and drinks on a later trip to Edinburgh. In those days people thought Edinburgh a better Festival to be seen in even than Brighton. It felt like a good career move. But not as good as the lead in 'Base Instinct'.

She was walking past a high wall and towards wrought-iron gates. She didn't know if the house inside lived up to them, but she assumed it did, though no stars-tourist had ever been inside. This was the house where Sharon Stun lived: Sharon, who had once occupied the bedsit opposite Mary Cecilia Bruin. Pervhoven had suggested she test for 'Base Instinct'. He said it would be a raunchy movie, but there were three big roles for women. She got to test for the leg-crossing scene in the leather mini-skirt. She'd been surprised that Sharon had tested without a G-string, as Sharon had been surprised that she kept hers on. Then had come an urgent offer: we're in at Edinburgh. She hesitated: it was between her, Sharon, and Treena Jinglehorn for the lead. Sharon had said: 'May the least knickers win!' Then Mary actually read the script, and wondered, did she really want to play a nymphomaniac, necrophiliac nudist who killed her lovers with a dagger of ice? Could such a film be a success? She missed the final screen-test. When she got back from Edinburgh flat broke and behind with the rent, Pervhoven was angry and putting it round that she was 'difficult'.

She almost ran past the iron gates and CC-cams of Sharon's house: she didn't want her old audition queue mate to see what had become of her. It had been Sharon who got her into the film as her body-double. And being a body-double had convinced her that although she wouldn't do prostitution or even porno, she could perhaps work at the LappyCat Club, which had kept her alive for the last two years.

Just after Mary passed the gates, they swung open almost silently. A vast limo came out, engine quiet as the purr of a kitten, quieter than the crunch of tyres on the gravel. It turned up the hill and started to pass her slowly on the other side of the road. It was Sharon's car, but it would only contain bodyguards. Sharon would be running beside it, in fact Mary should have been able to see her over the roof, but turned away. If she called out, Sharon might stop, and perhaps be touchable for a loan, but what would be the point? Mary was past even being a body-double, not for a star who would be running all the way to the studio atop the Downs.

She walked slowly till the car and the running Sharon were out of sight. She was more convinced with every step that the hill really was the Devil's work. What was the legend, that he had wanted to let the sea rush in though a gap in the Downs and flood Sussex? Midsummer's Day came into it, some local fantastical twaddle. Oh yes, the devil thought Midsummer's Day was an old pagan feast, a propitious time to finalise his work, but he saw a lit candle shining from an ancient church, St Coelmund's in the North Laine Saxon enclave in Brighton, and fled in terror.

Mary passed the point where the by-pass ran down the former Woodland Drive to the town. Beyond, apart from a few token trees left standing, it was movie sets and studio buildings, all part of the Hove Woods conglomerate. H-Woods had been flourishing since 'Base Instinct' broke records. Mary walked on and on, past trailers and star-caravans and sets, a giant blue phone-box in a launching-gantry, two cardboard castles, a generic space-alien building. It was easier here, she was on the plateau which formed the top of the Downs. The former golf clubhouse, now a Director's Club; Mary Cecilia didn't know any hot director apart from Pervhoven, and he'd been cooling since 'LappyCats the Movie' flopped. Mary knew why it had done badly. Pervhoven had a perfect chance to cast in the lead role Boady Blue herself, a talented actress who was also a real LappyCat. It would have made both their careers. Instead, he had given her a brief screen-test at an hour so early even Sharon would scarcely have pulled on her running shoes. She had done well at the club the night before, been bought lots of drinks, wasn't quite at her best. In fact the movie hadn't been as bad as the crits implied. Mary had been dragged along by the girls from the club expecting to hate it, but found it was no sexier than 'Base Instinct' but a lot less violent. It had seemed to her as good a portrait of the cynical gambling city of Port Sladas as Sharon's Amber Cup-winning 'Gambling Den'. What it had lacked was an actress...the Aussie soap star Pervhoven had cast as lead didn't ring enough bells to save it Somehow the word had got out that Mary had auditioned and not even got to double for one of the many bodies. It simply hadn't been true that she was drinking too much then. Appreciative customers simply bought her lots of drinks.

Now she could see the sign from behind. The red sun was above the horizon now, and would be glittering off the gold front. It was a spectacular morning to show up the directors who had so often humiliated her in the LappyCat years. Mary had never been so close to the sign. The letters were huge, and not as near to the sharp scarp of the down as she had hoped. It would never do to just be injured. She thought of lying broken-limbed on the flat before the sign until some busybody found her and called an ambulance. She almost ran back to Brighton, but she was past running. She was no Sharon Stun, she knew that now.

The flat area was narrowest in front of the first letter 'O'. There'd been some kind of landslip there. She would just have to jump well. She left her holdall with its identifying resume between the 'O' and the'V'. She noticed the sign was made of a complex mix of reflective and prismatic strips, presumably so it was illuminated by the sun from behind during the day, as it had been designed mainly to be seen by those approaching from the north. At the moment, however, the red dawning sun was catching it direct. There was a ladder, presumably for use by cleaners, attached to the back of each letter.

As Mary Cecilia started to climb, she could see the red warning light of the Midsummer sun suffused through the material of the sign. Her scholls were now very uncomfortable so she kicked them off and, at once feeling liberated, climbed swiftly on till she reached the top of the 'O'. Luckily, the letters were three-dimensional and she was able to sit and take a breath before dying. From here, she could not see Brighton or Hove, only the flat land of Mid-Sussex which the devil had wanted to drown. The air was clean and cool in her aching lungs, the sun was red and the sky getting bluer. It was a good morning to be alive, and a good one to die, if living was not what you were good at. She had to make herself up. She got out the mascara, but every time she went to apply it to her eyes, they filled with tears. She remembered the family who deeply loved someone else they wanted her to be, the childhood pets who had all died, the friends who had lost touch, the lovers who had peeled away as her career and her body started to sag. No one, not even Sharon, least of all herself, liked her as she was. They all wanted her to be more successful, or just totally different. She had no handkerchiefs, or even tissues. She got out the pencil-lipstick, and tried to outline her lips without the aid of a mirror.

While she was doing this, she gradually became aware of an unpleasant sulphurous smell, of voices from below her, and an odd sound like a cross between a chop and a slurp. For a second she panicked: she supposed it was technically illegal to climb the sign, even for the purpose of jumping off it. Then she calmed down and reflected that having someone around might be an advantage. The one flaw with the jumping plan was that if no one saw her go, her body might wind up somewhere where no one would find it till it was beyond recognition. She looked cautiously over the edge of the 'O'.

Two male figures stood directly below her. The odd noise was caused by one of them digging with what looked like a garden fork. He seemed to be shovelling earth into the landslip gap; the very point into which she had planned to leap. He was oddly dressed in a top hat and tails. His trousers, boots and coat-tails were heavily splattered with dirt from the digging he was doing. The other wore a dark suit and had kept it clean by standing well away from the digger. He carried a palmtop computer and was saying:

'This looks a totally non-productive exercise!' The dirty digger ignored him and carried on digging inefficiently with his fork. She realised he was right in her jump path. If she leaped while he was working, she might land on top of him, even impale herself on the fork. She shuddered at the thought. She called out:

'Excuse me! Could you move aside for a minute!'

The clean observer gave her a very cold look and said:

'Another unproductive soul! Can't you put her off?' The dirty digger looked up. His face was lined and skeletal. His eyes were old as a glacier, cold as a dagger of ice. He looked tired, as tired as if he had started digging in Australia, and dug his way all through the bowels of the Earth to reach the Dyke. Oddly, he had what looked like corks hanging from the brim of his hat. He said:

'My dear, I have no intention of moving until I have repaired the damage to my...work. And let me assure you, that if and when you make a suicidal leap, your soul will belong to me for ever.'

Mary shuddered again. Before she could think of anything to say the clean observer cut in. 'That's exactly what I mean! The bottom line is, you're collecting totally unproductive souls. Look at this one! Some kind of actress obviously, but not one who's starred in any product, let alone shifted any.'

The dirty digger lifted his hat slightly and looked her up and down. 'Hmm, she's pretty enough to be a possible. Nice body, though she obviously succumbs to the temptations offered by the world. But can she act, Mr Beal?'

Mary Cecilia said indignantly: 'I've been in several films!'

'But will the next few be more productive than the last?' The clean observer said. 'That's the bottom line!'

She hesitated. 'I... I'm resting between projects right at the moment.'

The dirty digger nodded. 'Obviously.' He hesitated. 'You know, collecting souls has always been my core business, Mr Beal. Why can't I have this one? Assuming,' and he tipped his hat at Mary. 'That she does decide to jump!'

Mary decided to give it a little longer. She didn't believe these two were really supernatural beings, but they might be eccentric millionaires. Meanwhile, Mr Beal was waving his palmtop and shouting.

'Because you're over-extended in several fields of low-yield souls! Just look at your political portfolio! Three hundred assorted back-bench MPs, twenty low-grade junior ministers, the three cabinet members no one's ever heard of! They'll be a complete waste of furnace space! And as to what happened to your collection of hereditary peers...'

'Very well, very well!' The devil looked at Mary, and he said: 'My dear, I have to insist you refrain from jumping until we have considered what investment we might make in you. And for that I'm afraid I now have to consult Liz. To the Devil, a daughter can sometimes be a hindrance. Lizzie! Come!' Mary was willing to delay jumping, but had not got where she was by obeying the orders of men in black suits. She decided she would look more serious if she stood up, but found her bare thighs seemed to be stuck to the sign-top on which she was sitting. She panicked for an instant, and then continued to panic. She had been too long in Brighton, and was starting to believe the fantastical New Age twaddle which was the downside of life there. She had drunk too much, and was paralysed and starting to hallucinate.

As if to confirm her fears, her nostrils filled with a bizarre smell, as if someone had mixed Chanel No 9 with brimstone. A woman had joined the others. She wore a tight black catsuit tucked into long black boots. Her face was pale and so was her hair. She exclaimed indignantly:

'I was walking about in the world, planning my next deal!'

The dirty digger said: 'Sorry, my dear, but we need to consult you on an investment problem. This suicidal young woman is, er...'

'Mary Cecilia Bruin.' Mary was not paralysed, just stuck like a fly to the sign. She seemed to freeze, however, as the black-clad devilette, or whatever she was, gave her a look almost as cold as her father's, but then said:

'Liz Luce-Fire, Vice-President, World Communications. I think I know you.'

'You do?' Mary gasped, amazed.

'You were the Unicorn Girl in 'Do Androids Dream of Electric Sheep?'.'

'I was... that's brilliant! My part was cut from the Director's cut!'

The dirty digger laughed. 'My dear, when we take over, you won't find mere directors cutting pretty things like you from our movies!'

'But I thought... you... people, ran pretty much everything round here anyway!'

The clean observer, Mr Beal, said: 'So far, we're just freeholders. But that has to change. When we take over the studio...'

'What, Hove Woods?'

'Well, we're starting with Nineteenth Century Folks. We'll be updating it to Twenty One CF.'

The dirty digger cut in: 'We'll shake it up and make it a tearaway studio with lots of tit!'

Mary Cecilia remembered she was a LappyCat, and qualified to provide some of that tit. She said cautiously:

'Er, what sort of films will you make?'
They all answered at once. Liz Luce-Fire said:
'Market leaders!'
Mr Beal snapped:
'Sound bankable projects!'
The dirty digger shouted:
'Big booming blockbusters to take on the Americans and wipe the floor with them! Asteroids destroying the Earth! James Bond on rocket sleds! Cemi Moira as a LappyCat! Willy Brucis saving the world!' They all laughed loudly at that. Mary considered her position. She could die, if she could unstick herself from the sign, and not even make it into the digger's soul collection, or she could sign up for what sounded like a down-market but exciting project. She said:
'Just what do you want from me?'
They looked at each other. Liz said:
'I think you can do it. We offer a seven year stardom contract. To the right actress. All we want in exchange is a deed signed in blood assigning your soul to us. Your body you keep for your own... usage.'
'For seven years?'
'Renewable. If you still shift product after seven years, you get another seven. You'd be surprised how long some of our contractees have been on our books.'
Sweat was running out of every pore of Mary's skin. She realised the moisture had unstuck her thighs from the sign, and at the same time that she was going to accept the offer. She had vowed never to sell her body, but she had always known her soul might have to go.

She jumped up, and not fancying going back down the ladder, noticed that the nearest arm of the 'V' ran over the shoulder of the 'O' she was on. She was suddenly full of energy: she ran over and jumped lightly onto the top of the 'V' arm. From there it was easy to slide down the inner slope of the 'V'. She came to rest with an unpleasant bump in the cleft of the 'V'. That cleared her mind, and she said:
'Shouldn't I discuss this with some, er, agent?'
Mr Beal was printing a contract from his palmtop. Liz Luce smiled evilly and handed it up to Mary.
'I think you'll find we have all the more successful agents.'
Mr Beal shouted: 'And all the rest! We have to downsize that portfolio.'
Liz just shrugged. Mary sat in the cleft of the 'V' and panicked. To sign, she had to shed her own blood, and she hated the sight of it. She spent her periods in a permanent faint. She had never dared audition for hospital soaps or vampire movies. Merely the thought of blood was making her head swim, making the world circle. The morning light was still red... not the red of blood, the red of a warning.
After she signed, Mary felt too weak to get out of the cleft of the 'V'. Eventually, she handed the contract down to Liz Luce-Fire, who spared it the briefest of glances and popped it into a black bag. The demonette said:
'Your first project will be 'The Trumanator'. The concept is, a cross between 'The Truman Show' and 'The Terminator'. You'll play a girl whose life is really an SF TV

serial. She has to decide which of two aliens from the future has to make her pregnant, and which, obviously, wants to terminate her. We've lined up some big names.'

'Er, Benny Cranach? Rick Allman?'

'None of that! Will you believe, Smarmy Farcensnigger!'

Mary C slipped off the back of the 'V' cleft and wandered away from her new employers. She had been given a platinum card, some scholls that fitted, and a roll of suspiciously crisp fivers. She felt surprisingly good. She walked till she reached the Directors' Club.

On the steps, a press event was taking place. Two women in leather mini-skirts identical to her own were handing out fruit-flavoured ice daggers to the journalists. She recognised Sharon Stun and Treena Jinglehorn. Sharon waved her over.

'Hi Mary. We're just doing pre-pub for 'Base Instinct 2'.

She gave a grapefruit ice dagger to Mary, who said:

'What, you're reprising your role?'

'No, Treena this time. I'm just producing.'

The crowd was starting to disperse. Sharon said:

'We must do brunch. My place?' Her limo was cruising up, and she steered Mary and Treena towards it. 'Don't worry, I only run uphill!'

As soon as they were settled in the back of the limo, Sharon said:

'So, what's happening? No one hears a word about you for two years, then suddenly you're the next big thing at 19CF. What's the secret?'

She tactfully hadn't mentioned the various LappyCat fiascos. Sharon had a burning desire to be number one, but found life lonely at the top, and wanted her old pals to be numbers two and three. Mary realised Sharon was the nearest thing she had to a friend, and started to tell her all about the Digger, Mr Beal, and Liz Luce-Fire. Sharon whistled. 'The Digger, eh? Your soul! I only had to contribute my body to advance my career, and I got it back in reasonable shape. Mind you, there are a lot of Devil stories in Brighton. Most of them say he's drawn back to the Dyke every Midsummer's Day. It's not a good day for him. You should listen to the locals. They know what they're talking about. Mind you, they say it's never a good idea to sign a contract with him, especially if you sign it in blood.'

Treena exclaimed:

'Mary-C, surely you hate blood! Didn't you faint during the killing scene at the premiere of 'Base' and get carried out?'

'That's right!' Sharon said. 'Your tits were out of your cleavage, and you were out of everything! Come to think of it, you passed out on the set!'

She explained to Treena, who had played the shrink, and not been needed for the actual sex-murder scenes: 'She went out cold every time they sprayed her with tomato juice. In the end, I had to body-double for myself!'

They both looked expectantly at Mary, almost hopefully. Mary wondered if they were hoping she hadn't signed in blood, or just that the contract would fall through and she wouldn't become a star. They didn't know she had intended to kill herself that morning. She said:

'Well, when it came to signing, the sky was very red, I felt it was a warning, I felt really groggy, and I didn't know what to do. Then I remembered I had a red lipstick-pencil, so I signed in that. Do you think that'll do?' At once she wondered if they had sold their own souls, and would betray her. But Sharon said:

'No! I think you've signed a contract with the Devil he can't hold you to!'

'But what if... the films they promised... if I can't hold them to those!' 'Oh, I doubt they'll notice. Not on Midsummer morning. But if they do, someone's made a collection of all the fabulous stories people tell about Brighton. We've got the film rights. This story ought to be in it, and so ought you.'

'Fabulous Brighton!' Mary Cecilia breathed. And for the first time since she reached Brighton, she started to believe it.

Fabulous Brighton: The Authors

Nigel Brown: Nigel has had science fiction, fantasy and ghost stories published in the UK and USA.
Deirdre Counihan: a long term resident of Brighton, Deirdre is the Art Editor of Scheherazade magazine and a well known local artist and writer.
Elizabeth Counihan: Liz is the Editor of Scheherazade magazine, and has been published in Interzone and the Mammoth Book of Seriously Comic Fantasy, among others.
Christopher Enby: Christopher is a local artist and writer.
Peter T. Garratt: Peter is a writer of SF, Fantasy, Historical and other detective fiction. He is a psychologist and Arthurian, who was born and bred in Brighton. His work has been featured in Interzone and many other magazines, and he has appeared in numerous anthologies of short fiction, including 'Shakespearean Detectives' and 'Shakesperean Whodunnits.'
Peter James: Peter is a well-known and widely published horror writer, whose novels include 'Host', 'Faith' and 'Prophecy.'
Paul Laville: Paul is a former music journalist. This is his first appearance as a fiction writer.
Larry Matthews: Larry Matthews has written numerous articles for technical journals and magazines but this is his first published short story. He lived in Brighton for the last two decades of the recent millennium.
Nick Szczepanik: is a football writer for the Times.
Lynne Truss: novelist, playwright, broadcaster and journalist, Lynne is a sports columnist for the Times and author of the bestselling 'Going Loco' and other novels.
Liz Williams: A local author, Liz has had work featured in Asimov's Magazine, Interzone, and The Third Alternative among others. She has also had a short story featured in Gardner Dozois' 16th Year's Best Science Fiction.
Veronica Williams: a widely published Gothic novelist (novels include 'Merlinston', 'Wildashe' and 'A House in Shadow').

Good luck to *FABULOUS BRIGHTON*

AUSTIN GRAY are sponsors of Peter James' story, "12 Bolinbroke Avenue"

SCH